And Chocolate Shall Lead Us

by

Lew Hollander

Produced in the UNITED STATES OF AMERICA.

Authored by LEWIS E. HOLLANDER, JR.

Designed and Illustrated by EAGLE LADY DESIGN STUDIO.

Published by GREEN MANSIONS, INC., P.O. Box 100, Redmond, OR 97756

Cover and Illustrationst:

Designed and Illustrated by EAGLE LADY DESIGN STUDIO

ISBN 0-9728156-1-9

Books by Lewis E. Hollander:

And Chocolate Shall Lead Us

And Chocolate Shall Lead Us (for children)

Endurance Riding, From Beginning to Winning

For ordering books:

GREEN MANSIONS, INC.

P.O. Box 100, Redmond, OR 97756, U.S.A.

www.andchocolateshallleadus.com

www.lewhollander.com

Book Stores and Retail Stores:

Order wholesale directly from IngramSpark

Acknowledgement

The author would like to acknowledge Heather Meyers, whose brilliance in giving life to the characters and excitement to the story has made the book possible, to Crystal McCage, for editing the book and converting it to English, and to Sandra Jones of Eagle Lady Design Studio, whose illustrating genius and organizing skills gave the book color and brought it to fruition.

Thank you for the help.

Preface

The theory of DOMINANCE was essential for evolution to deliver us to the age of enlightenment. Now, we are at a crossroads; either we abandon dominance or be destroyed as a species. I attempt, through fiction, to reveal these truths about modern society, for as Shakespeare said, "Many a truth is said in jest." It is my hope that with the help of a 100,000 year old probe from Venus, you can see not only our inevitable self-destruction but also a solution. Through this alien entity, a solution for survival exists with a new set of Ten Commandments and a new vision of a world free of war, poverty, and oppression. The hope for the solution lies within our hearts, and the power to succeed lies in our resolve to abandon dominance. To the adherents, the patriots, the company men, the followers, and the leaders, try, as you read this book, to look all the way to the conclusion before dismissing its thesis. By this story, I have attempted to get your attention. I make no claim for scientific accuracy and in some cases have stepped into fantasy to make my point. I hope through this book to take a small step toward a new world order that would give us peace on Earth, teach us respect for each other, and eliminate the malediction of dominance. True, the achievement of these noble goals will require a total change of our social system, but the alternative is unthinkable. What have we got to lose? If I could only open one set of eyes, broaden the view of one mind, teach one person tolerance, or break just one link in the chain of dominance, this book would be a success.

Contents

Illustrations

CHAPTER I (VENUS)

Going to Hell

The dying embers of a once great society smolder towards extinction under a dead planet's soil, telling a dark story of a people who destroyed themselves. It is 190,786 of the Venusian calendar, or approximately 100,000 BC in Earth chronology. While the current surface temperature leaps to temperatures of over 300 Celsius (572 F), a few survivors remain on this formerly beautiful and temperate planet, trapped deep underground in small subterranean colonies. In recent years, communication has become exceedingly difficult between the colonies due to the ever-pressing need to dig deeper as the surface temperature continues to rise. Fortunately, the Venusian forefathers stock-piled a large amount of nuclear, fissionable material which is now being used as the only energy source to cool and light these underground communities. While the supply of energy is limited, a bigger threat to survival exists for the Venusian survivors. Returning to the surface now is impossible because of the extreme conditions of high pressure and heat. The Venusians must retreat deeper and deeper into the planet's crust, unfortunately becoming increasingly closer to the internal heat of the planet. They are trapped between the surface heat and the internal heat. Without a cooling system, they will be cooked alive.

Locked in this inexorable hell, in a small windowless chamber, a scientist, Jonic, his mate Nadia, and their male offspring named Kylia, all live, work, and commiserate about how it is now and once was. Their small but neatly kept apartment seems like it would lend itself to a comfortable existence with its running water, sewer, electricity, and the all-important cool air supply. But it is not the confined quarters and reduced living standards that cause the Venusians their heartache. More, it is the hopelessness of their situation. The surface temperature of Venus is rising irreversibly as properly predicted by scientists thousands of years ago. The trapped civilization is kept alive only by dangerously over-worked cooling systems. In the back of every Venusian's mind is the understanding that survival is only temporary, leading to a very depressing and dismal portent for the future.

But, despite this knowledge of their impending demise, Jonic and his family struggle to make their current existence at least worthwhile. They attempt to continue in their routines, hoping the distraction will replace the feelings of hopelessness. Although there is little room in the subterranean colonies for schools, libraries, shops, and recreation, Nadia enjoys taking her son to the central hydroponics garden, a garden which provides the food supply and also serves as a meeting hall, recreation center, play ground, commons, and amusement park. Unfortunately, the danger of leaving the apartment makes it a rare occasion when the family can venture out, but for Nadia and Jonic, sometimes it is an acceptable risk to see the smile on Kylia's face. Most of the time, however, the danger is too great, and most items are delivered. The majority of Venusians prefer the delivery system. The thrill of shopping fades when the shops carry only necessities and a few craft items produced with the select elements available so far underground.

But despite being almost permanently locked into their home, Jonic and his family find joy in the excellent communication they have within their community via computer. The computer serves as a window to the outer world and is their voice. All the children play with other children via the computer. They create or recreate, by virtual reality, the scene as it once was in greater days on the surface. Kylia uses computers to experience the bright sky, the colorful flowers, and the towering trees. His favorite pastime is to look up views of nature, like those once so familiar scenes of mountains and lakes. All these are gone forever but the children of the community love to see the long lost beauty. Here, and only here, they can view and experience through simulation life as it used to be, or maybe better, as it should have been.

Jonic can't help but feel a pain in his heart when he watches his child stares wide-eyed at the computer screen. Jonic knows his child will never experience the wonder of the planet as it once was. He remembers his initial excitement at receiving a child permit, a circumstance most unusual due to the tight control of the population density. His good fortune came because he is considered a "needed one," as he possesses skills essential to the survival of the community. He is a thermodynamicist, specializing in the nuclear cooling system and has invented a number of ingenious methods to keep the system operating efficiently and reliably. He has had a profound influence on the community. His wife, Nadia, also serves the community well as an entertainer and educator for youngsters. So, because of

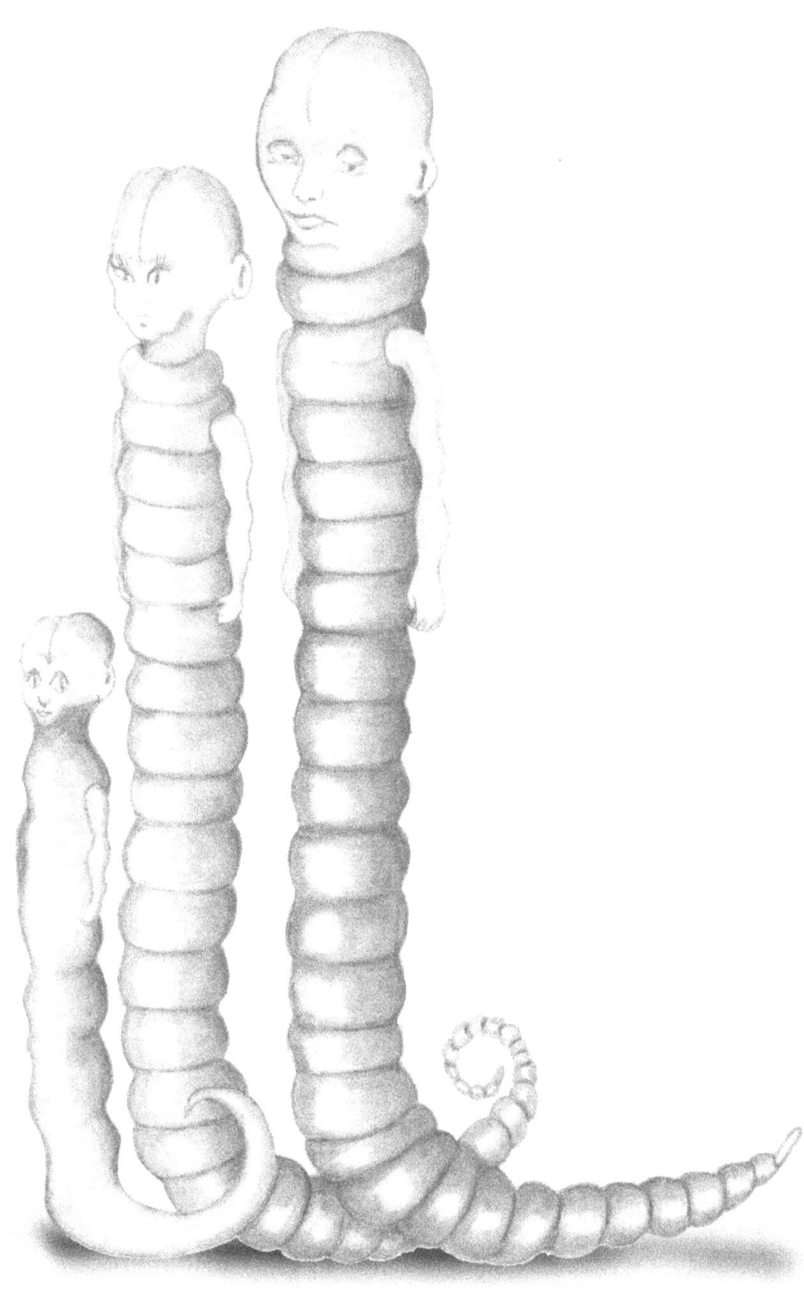

The Venusian Family

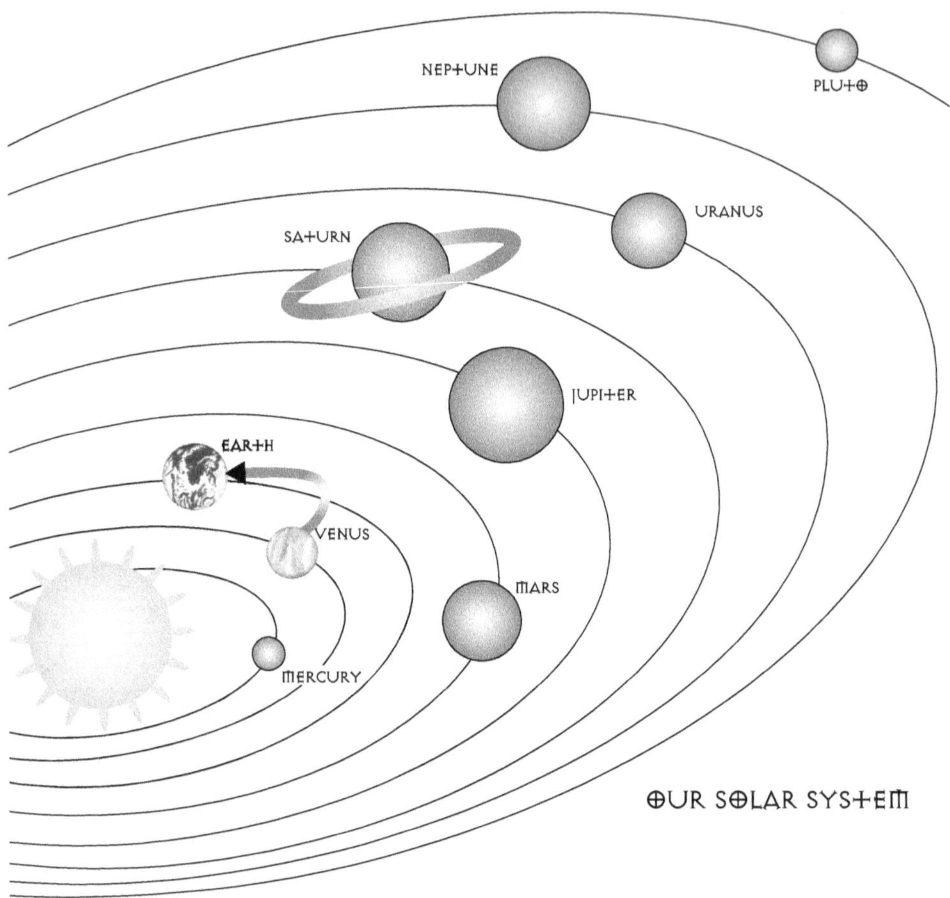

their necessity to the community, Jonic and Nadia received the special privilege of harvesting a child.

The process of having children, like everything else, became dramatically different when the Venusians moved underground. The population needed to be redesigned for the underground world they were about to enter. Biology labs worked overtime on the redesign of beings for sub-surface living. The deteriorating conditions on the surface allowed little time to accomplish this difficult task. Fortunately, the population had already used genetic engineering to improve the species and most females no longer carried a fetus to term. Once a couple obtained all the necessary permits to have an offspring and the egg was fertilized, they would then deposit it at a fetal farm which consisted of rows and rows of fetuses, all growing in artificial uteruses under ideal nutritional conditions complete with massage, motion, and nurturing to simulate pregnancy. Once the fetus came to term, it was delivered to the proud parents for rearing. Jonic and Nadia's child was bred in this manner.

The advantages of this system were obvious. Nadia was freed from carrying this huge burden around all the time; any detrimental recreational habits did not impact the fetus, and any accidents that Nadia could not avoid would not hurt the fetus. This system yielded a miscarriage rate near zero, and there were no abortions. Parents had to show financial stability, ability to educate the child, and DNA which does not portend any problems or deformities. The genetically engineered children of the subterranean world have larger heads to accommodate a bigger brain and a smaller, more worm-like frame to enable them to maneuver through the subterranean tunnels lit only by low florescent lighting. Eyesight has been deemphasized and hearing improved. All the personnel have been sized the same so there was no longer large, small, and medium, just one size to fit the tunnels.

As Jonic looks at his specially bred tunnel child, he wonders if receiving the child permit was truly a blessing. What kind of life can children possibly have down here? He wants desperately to explain to all the children why they are denied the happiness of a surface life. But how can he explain what he himself has trouble understanding? How could this happen? As a scientist, he understands full well the how, the chemistry of the green house warming, but he does not understand the why. Scientists, for years, predicted this result, but when all was well on the surface, their warnings were ignored in favor of short-term profit and political, religious, and financial control. Jonic knew he had to at least try to explain. A few weeks ago, he found Kylia looking up "green house effect" on the computer. Jonic had never explained it, but the children of the community had certainly heard the term and were anxious to learn the sad history of their planet. Jonic knows its time and calls Klyia away from his virtual games and lets him know Jonic is ready to give the explanation he has been waiting to hear. Kylia looks up at his father intrigued, as he begins in his typical scientific fashion.

"I should have told you sooner, but I was somehow hoping I would never have to tell this terrible story. First, you must understand that the current surface of Venus has a thick, heavy (90 times that of Earth) atmosphere of 95% carbon Dioxide, 3.5% Nitrogen, and the rest is sulfur dioxide, argon, and carbon monoxide. The Earth, on the other hand, has 21% oxygen, 78% nitrogen, and only 1%

other gases, including carbon dioxide. But the Earth was not always this way," Jonic explains.

"Once, the Earth had a thick carbon dioxide and methane atmosphere. So both planets started off with excess carbon dioxide. Venus, being the second planet from the sun, was warmed by the sun, and life evolved there first. The Earth followed at a slower pace since it was the third planet. When life first came to Venus and Earth, it evolved in the form of cyanobacteria (blue green algae) which loved the excess carbon dioxide atmosphere and by the process of photosynthesis used the carbon dioxide and produced oxygen."

Jonic pauses to make sure Kylia has no questions, but there is no need as he understands this part completely. So Jonic continues.

"Gradually, over billions of years, the carbon dioxide of both planets was stored in the ground as what we now call fossil fuels like oil, natural gas, coal, and lignite. The atmosphere became oxidizing, enabling the evolution of species which relied on oxidation for an energy supply. In other words, animals of all sorts appeared. The plants continued to reduce the carbon dioxide and put out oxygen into the air. This was great for the animals that breathed this oxygen, and many varieties thrived, eventually giving rise to intelligent species, which were able to teach their young, and, by writing and libraries, store knowledge to pass down the accumulation of information. And this was called progress. The result was a civilization which became ever more complex. Now, the problem was that this civilization needed energy to drive its machines, keep warm, keep cool and produce goods and services. To do this they started to burn the fossil fuel supply buried in the ground. This, of course, reversed the process and, in a few hundred years, much of the carbon dioxide was returned to the atmosphere. This seemed to not be a problem because it encourages plant life and is colorless, odorless, and invisible. So you really do not know it is there in increasing amounts. NO WORRIES, right?"

At this, Jonic pauses, and Kylia waits anxiously. But Jonic feels he cannot go on. There is something about Kylia looking up at him while he tells the horrible story that makes him unable to continue. Maybe it's that he sees hope in his eyes when there really is none. Or maybe it's that he wants to save the children of the community from his pain. He sends Kylia away, knowing he will return with more difficult questions Jonic simply does not want to answer.

The Greenhouse Effect

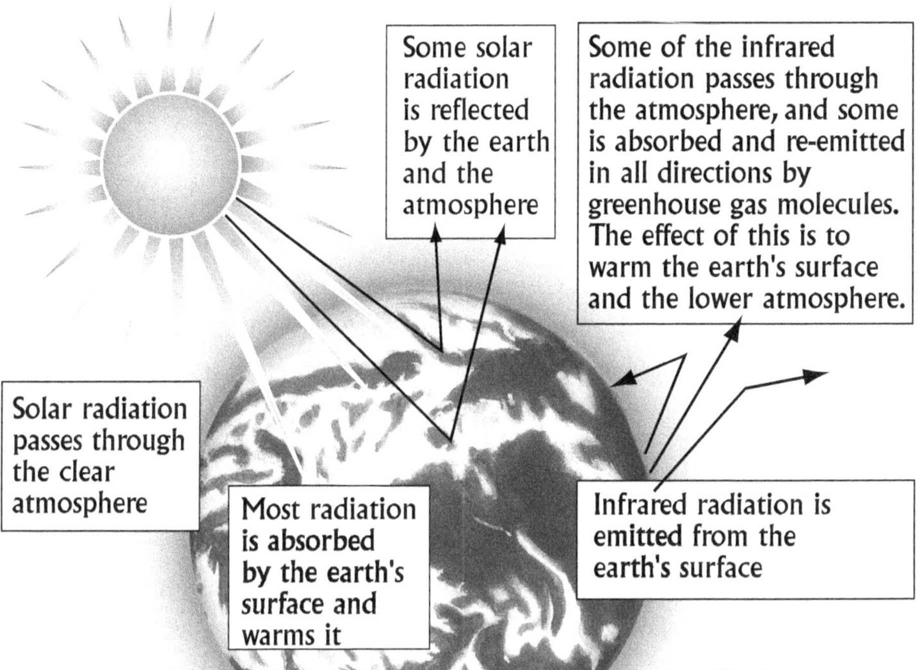

Klyia looks at his father and knows he shouldn't press on. Never has he seen his father with such a disturbed expression. Kylia knows his father needs some time to think, and so he returns to the beloved computer to find out more information, happy to have a new project to study in these otherwise boring caves.

"What should I look up?" Kylia thinks to himself. "What would tell me the rest of the story?"

Kylia really wants to hear the tales of how it was before the heat forced them into this hell. Adults talk about going to hell. Hell is a hot place and maybe you send yourself there. It looks like for this little community that hell is just where they are going.

On his computer, Kylia remembers looking up the "green house effect" a few weeks ago. He remembers how upset his father was and knew this must be the way to the explanation. He types in "green house effect."

"This is what made our life so miserable and hopeless," he says.

The computer spews out lots of facts and figures. He quickly learns that this effect allows the sun's infrared, heat rays to penetrate the Venusian's atmosphere, but, after incidence with the surface, a portion is reflected back into space. With industrialization and the introduction of air pollution, certain gases, notably carbon dioxide, absorb the reflected heat rays, and thus, the sun's heat is retained by the planet. This process has always been going on. In modern times, however, energy generation became a more and more important commodity. As the society became more technologically dependent, the need for energy became greater.

Kylia can immediately see the dim prospects ahead and decides he must know why this had to happen. With all the technology available, someone must have seen this thing coming. If it so obvious to children, adults certainly would have recognized the problem. Unable to withhold his curiosity, he races to his father who is still sitting quietly where he left him.

Jonic sighs at the sight of his eager child. He knows he must finish the story but searches madly for delay. He hurriedly spurts out, "I think we need a break. Let's get some goodies from the Vendor-Pneumatic." Jonic knows that his child can not resist a treat and is glad to have a few extra moments to compose himself before he continues. Kylia welcomes the distraction, treats are few and far between in the caves and they love the Vendor-Pneumatic. The Vendor-Pneumatic is a wonderful gadget that takes orders and fills them via pneumatic tubes running throughout the entire community, a sort of store on tubes. Larger articles are sent in pieces, so everything is made to fit the maximum tube size. This is the ultimate shopping mall. All mail and messages also come this way because the family only leaves the home for special occasions, which requires police protection or the guard service. One of the real highlights of this sequestered existence is the sugar store. On the Vendor-Pneumatic, there is a wonderful commodity called chocolate which is dripped over all kinds of interesting things. Kylia orders the chocolate and his father looks on as he licks the last drops from his claw tips.

The delay is over and the story must continue. Jonic knows that chocolate cannot begin to ease the pain of the story he must tell. His child cannot possibly understand how all this was allowed to happen. Jonic too, as a scientist, is perplexed to explain why, when so much evidence was available, that those in charge went on for their personal profit to burn fossil fuels and not switch to cleaner sources like nuclear, hydro, solar, and wind power. It was because the leaders were also owners and distributors of the fossil fuel supply. Arguing against the power industry, who also owned the media and communication facilities, was almost hopeless. So the voters and the rest just went along. The carbon dioxide was colorless and had no smell and no taste, so the emissions from the power plants appeared to be clean. But everyone knows the products of combustion are carbon dioxide and water vapor. Gradually, the levels were bound to build and return the atmosphere to a carbon dioxide rich environment, resulting in a dramatic rise in surface temperature. But many leaders and owners of the gas, oil, and coal companies made huge profits and were able to keep control right up to the end. Even when the weather started to change and all knew something was wrong, they kept right on burning. By that time, it would not have made any difference as once the cycle of rising temperature starts it would be impossible to reverse in a reasonable time period. Yes, the story is an awful one, one that Jonic wishes he did not have to tell. How do you explain to a child that greed took away their chances of a happy surface life? How can Jonic tell his child that people did know what was happening but didn't stop and that the energy czars funded environmental movements which opposed the use of competitive nuclear technologies? But the worst part of the story for Jonic, the part that tears at his soul the most, is that there were viable solutions to fix what the greedy had done. One of the energy czars' arguments against the use of nuclear fuels was the problem with the disposal of the radioactive waste. The two environmental needs are clean air and clean water. So all excess radioactive products must be put in a location isolated from the water table and contained so there is no airborne potential. This is fairly easy to do with sturdy containers placed in areas that are not exposed to underground water flows such as deserts. Certainly, the threat from radiation was minimal compared to the total destruction of the environment caused by burning fossil fuels. Also, with radioactive contaminants, very accurate monitoring can be done and, even if some were to escape, which would be unlikely, it could easily be detected and filtered. And again, the filtration could be accurately monitored. But there was a campaign against nuclear energy. Solar, wind, and hydro are all really solar power. They are none pullulating and very useful, but for a technologically developed planet, the energy use quickly exceeds the total solar output incident on the planetary surface. Using the entire surface would seriously limit food production, greatly reduce the livability of the surface, and still not meet the energy needs of the society. The energy czars, by the use their power, money, and influence or dominance, discouraged not only nuclear energy, but public transportation and impeded bicycle and foot travel in favor of less efficient and more polluting fossil fuel vehicles.

Someday, Jonic will tell the whole story. For now, with the chocolate still drying, Jonic decides to skip the explanation of the greedy and begins to tell how they came to be locked underground. He knows this will appease Kylia and he would learn more of their history without being exposed to the wickedness of the former surface world. Jonic began again. "As the results of the global warming became apparent and time was running out, a massive underground project was commenced. A new government was organized, and for the first time, the government's prime objective was to SERVE the people. The past leaders, the greedy, the ignorant and their collaborators were all severely punished, and they and some of their offspring were not granted permits to reside in the new underground project. The life span on the surface, at that time, was still normal but there was no hope for any succeeding generations. An aggressive space program was initiated to propagate the species to the third planet and to send a record in the form of probes to recount the life and history of the people of Venus. The probes were to serve as a time capsule of sorts to be there when and if the transplanted species actually evolved into a technologically advanced society and wanted to know from whence they came. For the first time in the history of the planet, the people took a serious interest in the operation of their government, and they voted every day on everything."

Kylia is really interested in learning about the probes that were launched to neighboring planets. He questions his father and learns that there apparently had been an on-going series of experiments to locate other habitable planets. The third planet, Earth, seemed the most likely candidate for habitation. Apparently, a whole series of experiments with the mammalian life and fertilization by Venusian's sperm cells had proven successful and a new being had evolved from this experiment. Then, probes were sent to explain where the inhabitants had come from and what fate had befallen the second planet, Venus. Kylia has thousands more questions but the clock indicates that it is nighttime and his curious mind must be laid to rest. Jonic, relieved that he has appeased his child and excited him by the story of the probes, relaxes a little in his chair. Nadia gets the boy ready and then beckons for her mate to come and put him to bed. They finally tuck him in and said goodnight, even though it never gets light or dark except with a switch.

(The Creator gave us a brain to think with and nuclear, hydro, and solar energy to run our world with.)

The Discovery

"We will return when the weather improves," shouts head scientist Josh Van Dever across the bitter snowstorm to his research team. They are not lost as they are surveyors on a quest. Team members quickly mark the investigation site and record the coordinates before they begin their treacherous journey back towards camp, several miles away. As the team makes its way across the rugged Antarctic plain, they find it difficult to contain their excitement. Today, they had finally made some progress in discovering the source of the "signal". The team had little luck so far and many feared the University would pull out of the project. After all, it had been a struggle to gather funding to locate the source of these strange, local electromagnetic fluctuations first observed several years ago. In 2008, under the leadership of Josh Van Dever, however, the University finally thought this anomaly of sufficient interest to send this team of researchers to the source of the "signal", a location across the Ross Ice Shelf about 1200 Kilometers south of McMurdo in extremely rugged country. But because of extreme conditions in Antarctica, the members of the research team have had only a few months in which to work and both their time and patience was starting to run out. Few have high hopes for a discovery today, with the snowfall increasing at an alarming rate, the day getting late, and the storm worsening by the minute.

The "signals", if one could call them that, have been rather difficult for the team to locate because they seem to repeat a precise, complex code at completely random emission times. The signal is weak; it was only first detected during an aerial oil exploration survey along the ice shelf. The electromagnetic field recorder picks up this strange signal over and over. An analysis of the data indicates it is a complex message of some type, emitted at random intervals. This would be odd in itself but, additionally, the pattern does not seem to resemble any known natural phenomenon. The signal is so weak that it was easily missed by earlier exploration surveys. Further, since the signal is emitted randomly, the team can only try to triangulate on the source when it is actually transmitted, which is the team's lucky break today. The team had constructed a grid of detectors and were waiting for the next transmission when someone cried, "There it is!" And the team now knows they were right on location. They quickly relocate their receiver to better focus in on the source in the event of another emission. But that is all the progress that can be made today due to the weather and the lack of any subsequent emissions.

It is a long walk back to the laboratory base camp, and Josh Van Dever is bursting with excitement. He can hardly wait to analyze the data, after which he learns they were indeed right on the source of the signals, plus or minus ten meters. But what Josh didn't expect to learn was that the emissions are emanating from what appears to be a point source of energy, located approximately five meters below the surface. Knowing that it will take considerable digging equipment to reach that depth in the frozen ground and that such will be nearly impossible to accomplish before the planned evacuation, Josh nervously contacts the University sponsors. To his surprise, the University decides to push on, as a second trip will not be possible because of budget constraints. Josh begins to wonder how much the University knows about the signals, most campaigns with this little hard evidence would have been cancelled already.

Josh informs his team of the good news, and all are nearly beside themselves with anticipation. For three days, while the storm persists, they proceed with the data analysis, and plans are made for the excavation. On the fourth day, the weather clears, and the team is full of excitement as members start off to the dig site. This time they bring a backhoe specially equipped for the ice and snow. They can now ride in style behind the hoe on sleds. First the area must be cleared and leveled. They hope for another emission in order to pinpoint the location more accurately. Radiation monitoring and biological and chemical measuring equipment are installed; the members of the team have no idea what they may encounter.

As the dig proceeds, another emission occurs, and the source is finally accurately located. The team breathes a sigh of relief, knowing this greatly reduces the dig area that needs to be searched. The size of the emitter can now be determined and is estimated to be only 75 cm by 20 cm by 20 cm. This small size surprises everyone and makes the diggers a little more cautious. The diggers are within a meter of the source now, and great anticipation is everywhere. Not one member of this frozen homesick team would trade this moment for anything.

The team moves slowly and carefully, and then, there is another signal emission. Through the debris, a faint light shines for the duration of the message. Josh lifts out the final few scoops of earth very carefully, and a small red cylinder, something like a World War II shell casing, is revealed in the ice, sitting there at an odd angle. The team, detailed and deliberate, carefully removes soil and ice samples and documents them for future study and age determination. There is a low-level nuclear radiation measured in the area, and the team is forced to take precautions. The shell itself is wrapped in heavy shielding and then inserted in a series of plastic containers, each of which contains disinfectant and is germ proof and air-

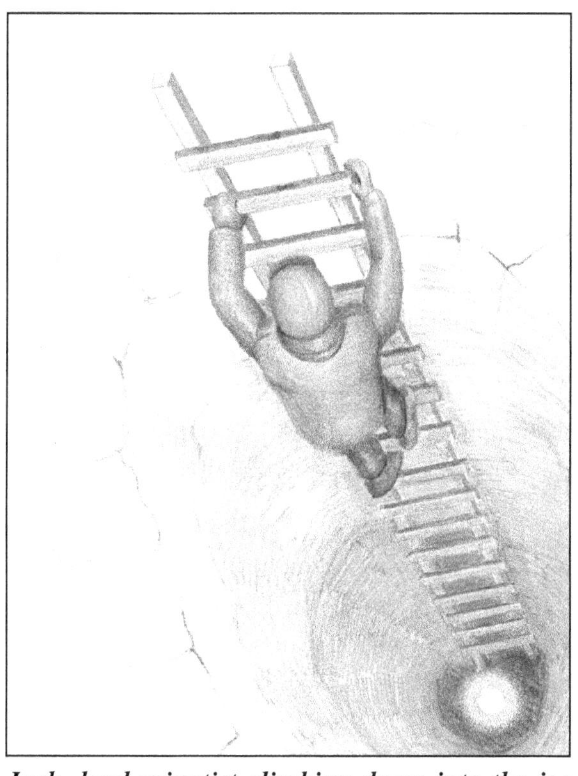

Josh, lead scientist climbing down into the ice hole where the probe is now exposed.

tight. They were designed to prevent any biological contamination or escape of toxic material. The team records the location and documents the site in the event a return trip is necessary to retrieve further parts or pieces of this missile. They dig all around the area but find no other pieces or parts to accompany the shell.

Josh Van Dever is having a difficult time controlling his excitement and his exuberant team. The crew, all dedicated scientists, carefully packages their little charge with the proper shielding and zoom back to the lab. The missile does appear to have a radioactive power source, but there is little external contamination. The team sets up photo cells to monitor the light emission and the already very familiar electromagnetic output. As Josh finishes setting up the final testing apparatus, he notices a plug at the rear of the shell which seems to require a special tool to fit. Josh and his teammates become frustratingly aware that the equipment in Antarctica will not suffice to even attempt to open the little fellow. They must wait until they return home to unlock any secrets of the device. It is decided to return home with this little fellow (the scientists had already grown attached to their discovery), the soil samples, and the survey data as quickly as possible.

Josh is so excited that he phones his wife by radio phone and exclaims that they may have found the first real encounter with an alien artifact. This would be one of the greatest discoveries of all time and he is a part of it. His two children get on the phone and ask when dad is coming home. He says he is on his way and looking forward to seeing them all.

The moment to leave arrives, but as excited as Josh is to get to a laboratory to continue studying the little fellow, he cannot bear to leave. He feels that he absolutely must return to the dig site once more to ensure that they have recovered everything, as it would be prohibitively expensive to return. The University, however, orders him to pack up camp and return as soon as possible. But Josh is a persistent, driven scientist and knows that he cannot be satisfied without one more search. There may be more probes or the vehicle that brought it here or a least parts of them. He asks his crew for volunteers to make one last trip to the site of the discovery. Everyone leaps at the opportunity. The team leaves immediately and conducts a thorough search. They find nothing in the area, but as good scientists, they have tried. Josh is dumbfounded. How can there be nothing more? His experience has taught him to expect surrounding evidence or additional clues. But, he and the team have confirmed that the missile is the only discovery to be made. Feeling as there is no other course of action, Josh gives the order to pack up the equipment and head for home.

On the voyage home, the University informs the research team that it has secured permission from the Department of Defense to use a remote desert laboratory that had previously been used for chemical and biological warfare research. They determined that this is the only place that will be secure enough to study the new find. The team is very excited as all realize this could be the find of the century or possibly the greatest find in history. The trip home is filled with great expectations. But Josh knows the team is bound to meet disappointment. There is simply too much at stake, and he wonders what the University expects from this find that causes them to involve the government. Or did the government involve itself? Josh knows only too well that University projects that become too important are often taken from the very people who pioneer them. And true to history, and not too much later, the University calls and instructs, then orders, and then threatens the team not to discuss this find with anyone. A final blow to the team occurred upon arrival at the University where the team members, with the exception of Josh, got reassigned to other duties, and the little missile is whisked off to the desert lab.

Of course, as the members of the research team became separated from their discovery, they grow angry. They developed an odd attachment to the little fellow, perhaps the most important discovery ever. And odder yet, the scientists somehow know that "The Messenger", the name they gave their discovery, contains important information for the whole of humanity. The public needs to know of the social importance of this find, and it seems to contradict the mission of the University to conceal this project in secrecy. Certainly, this does not befit an institution of higher learning. But no one listens to the complaints of the discoverers. The University makes complaints itself, having been relieved of command by the Army who recognizes the potential and the threat from a possible alien missile. Tests reveal that the missile landed at least 100,000 Earth years ago so the threat of attack is probably not eminent. But, more importantly to the government, the missile may contain interesting and useful technology that our government certainly does not want any other army to obtain. The Army assigns a "top secret" priority to the project.

CHAPTER III (EARTH)

The Little Fellow

All alone on a late Friday night, a weary but motivated researcher pours over the day's data one last time. This man, Lars Anderson, is no stranger to long hours, tedious work, and few rewards. He works as a leader in the field of investigation and communication with extraterrestrial life forms, an area of study that has consumed him since he was a child. For as long as Lars can remember, he has been fascinated with alien life forms and has devoted his life to listening to the universe just in case someone out there wished to contact us. He often sits there on these late nights with thousands of questions in his head. How will we recognize their signals? What frequency will they operate on? What forms will their transmissions be? Maybe in forms we will not understand. But, more importantly, if we do get a signal, how do we call back? How do we write rules for transmissions? It is this last question that is Lars' specialty. He has been working assiduously on the Search for Extra Terrestrial Intelligence, or the SETI program, and has been assigned to the Arecibo Space Station facility in Arecibo, Puerto Rico for the last few years. One of the goals of the station is to listen to space noise and look for intelligent life "out there." With a 300 meter dish antenna, the largest radio and radar telescope in the world, and sophisticated cryptographic computer capabilities, one might expect some sort of progress. Yet the data continues to yield few breakthroughs, and the work continues to be hard and somewhat boring. Lars is continually finding himself driven only by the prospects and possibilities of this endeavor. As another uneventful night draws to a close, Lars begins to pack up for home when the telephone rings.

Furiously packing for his new adventure, Lars can barely contain his excitement for what lies ahead. The telephone call was a job offer, an offer that Lars has dreamed of all his life. He is headed for a big change from his sequestered scientific life in Puerto Rico. He has been told of the great discovery in Antarctica and how his work as an extra terrestrial communications specialist makes him the most qualified person to work on deciphering the electromagnetic signal, opening, and figuring out the origin and mission of "The Messenger". Lars had never felt such joy. As he made his way from warm, tropical Puerto Rico to the dry desert of Nevada, he begins thinking of how he is going to organize the laboratory, hire the best scientific help available, and proceed with extreme caution to understand the little fellow. What a turn his life has made. If only he knew the many more that were to follow in the next year.

As Lars arrives in Nevada, he is driven to a secret laboratory in the desert. The laboratory is right up to date with the latest of everything. "The Messenger" has been placed in a vault type room beneath the surface within several sealed containers. The facility has been thoroughly cleaned and sterilized and ready for its new visitor. The laboratory was formerly used for biological and nuclear warfare and has the best isolation systems available. It was thought that its remote location gave some protection to the population should some hostile virus be set free on the world; although similar sites in the past have not always been successful in containing biological experiments. In fact, there were 50,000 dead sheep to attest to that at the Dugway Proving Grounds in Utah. The public was never made fully aware of the hazard anthrax imposed on them.

Once at the lab, Lars is given a tour of the facility and is relieved to see it meets his requirements; although he is taken a bit aback by the amount of security at the site. Towards the end of the tour, he is introduced to the only other scientist currently assigned, a Josh Van Dever. Apparently, Josh and his team had been the initial discoverers, and Josh has been providing the government with advice on the transportation and handling of the package. As Lars met Josh, he could see the familiar countenance of a man that had been separated from his loyal staff, a staff who undoubtedly braved the same harsh conditions of the discovery and had since been dismissed from their own study. Lars knows the situation only too well, the government proves less than sympathetic in matters it deems of great importance.

Lars is eager to begin the study of the little fellow. He knows he first needs a solid staff, and he needs to establish communication with the scientific community. Unfortunately, the governmental controls on the project are beyond what even Lars expected. He tries in vain to explain to the security force that a world-wide exchange and sharing of information is essential to proper scientific study. But his pleas are met only with reminders of his patriotic duties, and he is simply told to do his job and be quiet or be replaced. The security surrounding "The Messenger" is impenetrable especially since word got out that a major find has been made that

Nation Astronomy and Ionosphere Center, Arecibo Observatory.

it may be our first real communication with a past or alien civilization. In the cafes and living rooms throughout the world, people are excitedly wondering if the find means there was a past civilization possessing advanced technology or if there could really be a message from out there somewhere. The media leak is the government's worst nightmare, and it is thought to be payback from the disenfranchised University staff who are now forever separated from their discovery of a lifetime. First, it was just a hint of information. However, the rest of the story was soon revealed, and every television channel seemed to be telling about the discovery of a shell which emitted an electromagnetic signal and a faint light that was previously undetected in the depths of the Antarctic ice. The public knew that the shell had been taken to a laboratory in Nevada for government protection and study. However, it was also known that the US Army, who usually learns most of its top-secret information from CNN interviews, then knew it had something important that could either be a threat to the country or better, a new technology that would be beneficial in gaining superiority over an imagined enemy. That the military's interest was to improve its detection, destruction, and kill-rate capabilities rather than to share the knowledge of the little missile and help humanity was certainly no secret.

So, while the world discusses the find, argues the government's actions, and grew excited over the find, Lars tries to get to work in this fortress surrounded by elaborate security checks and a high-perimeter fence. The government assembles a staff of over fifty scientists, technicians, and administrators. Lars requests the original University team be assigned to the project, but the government refuses. Lars later hears rumors that the University has filed a law suit for compensation for the seizure of its property and the cost of recovery. Of course, this suit is classified "top secret," expunged from the court records, and settled out of court. The Department of Defense claims it's for national security. Lars is disgruntled at best, knowing that governments always think they know what is best for the people and are reluctant to inform the people of facts that are vital to their survival.

With this setback and a troubled mind, Lars does what he always does when things become troublesome; he decides to go on a long run. He remembers seeing in the paper that the Las Vegas Half Marathon was on this weekend, but he is unsure whether he really has the heart for it, given the current stress over the project. But he knows a good hard run seems to always help and decides he needs to run and to hell with the project. He packs his running shoes and heads to Vegas for a much needed break and a moment to collect his thoughts without having to go through six security check points.

Lars gets up early the day of the race, excited to feel like himself again. As he moves toward the starting line, his eyes catch those of a young lady who just fascinates him. Before he has chance to think, the run is on, and Lars feels his feet carry him toward the 10 mile mark. He is doing his best, but as the same young lady comes passing by, Lars gets a new incentive to run harder. He redoubles his efforts to stay with her and attempts to carry on a friendly conversation at the same time. Unfortunately, this is a considerable challenge as Lars' work has been consuming him, and he is not in the best of shape. He struggles to keep the pace.

"Boy this gal can really run", he thinks to himself as his legs start to burn.

He manages to stay close with her for the remainder of the half marathon and ends up getting his best time ever. Lars is amazed at how a lady can motivate him! Impressed by her and the inspiration she gave to him, Lars cannot help but approach her at the end of the race.

"That was quite a run," he remarks between gasping breaths.

"Yes. Felt great didn't it," she smiles with almost no effort.

"I don't suppose we could do this again sometime?" Lars asked nervously, hoping he had picked the right words.

"Sure. By the way, my name is Herdis. I'll be here for two more weeks, but you can call me when I get home."

Lars feels like he was floating on a cloud as he wrote down her number. A beautiful day, a beautiful woman with a wonderful name. Herdis. It was an old Danish name she told him. Old or new, it is a perfect name, and Lars finds himself repeating her name over and over in his head as he realized he had just experienced love at first sight. Not used to feeling this way, Lars tries desperately, in his scientific fashion to understand what had just occurred.

"Could this be happening to a scientist, a logical man, especially one with the responsibility of the world on his shoulders?" he asks himself.

"Can I live through the next two weeks until she returns to her home and I can at least talk with her?"

All the while, on the trip back to the Nevada facility, Lars can not think of much else but Herdis. He knows he has plenty to do. but he simply cannot stop thinking about her. This has never happened to him before, and it is really disturbing for him. True to his scientific nature, Lars always thought love was something that occurred through a very logical process of comparing likes, dislikes, life goals, sibling relations, parental histories, and so on. He had even compiled a list of all these things from studies of psychology journals and studies of successful sexual relationships. For example, an older sister of a younger brother should mate with a younger brother of an older sister. He had also studied the significant maternal and paternal effects on potential mates. He had even devised a rating scale for all the females he interviewed and kept charts of the results. He devised an equation for what he called the "permissible age gap." The equation included such things as physical disabilities, birth defects, intelligence, cultural background, and income potential. This way he could calculate the tolerable gap in age before domestic difficulties would occur. He thought every thinking person should do likewise in order to have a successful relationship.

But now, he is IN LOVE with a girl, and he doesn't even know her last name, shoe size, or sibling status! He doesn't understand how this could happen to a rational scientist like him, but somehow, he KNOWS he is in love, even without all the graphs and charts and data. There is no doubt of the symptoms of his affliction. Lars is beginning to feel overwhelmed. Life has seemed to change so quickly. Yesterday, he was a bored scientist analyzing uninteresting data in Puerto Rico, and now, now, he is in love and the head of the greatest scientific find of all times. What a change! He wonders if he can handle it all at once. He now suddenly has two loves, "the messenger" and this dream girl named Herdis. Lars hopes he can balance them both.

Back at the lab on Monday morning, Lars tries to focus on the project. He occupies himself by setting up lab facilities, getting clearances, and jumping through government hoops. He elicits the help of Josh Van Dever, who proves to be a huge help in getting things organized. Lars comes to depend on Josh and knows very well that the project could not have progressed without him. While they are working so hard to get the place ready, there is an underlying feeling from both the men. Both are very anxious to pay their full attention to the star visitor who remains in a secure, sealed, air tight, underground laboratory. Neither scientist has an idea what he will encounter upon opening the little fellow; although there is a general fear that it may involve strange germs, toxins, or explosives.

Finally, the day arrives, and preparations are underway to open the messenger. As Josh and Lars take the little fellow out of its vault, they glance nervously at each other. Where should we begin? They turn the missile over and discover a small port on the under side requiring a special tool to open it. Lars and Josh quickly realize that the required tool must be manufactured. Setbacks are all too familiar to the scientists, so they simply nod to one another and go about obtaining the tool. Drawings are made of the tool and sent to a manufacturer for a rush delivery. The security becomes increasingly oppressive and interferes with absolutely every action of the scientists. Lars would normally be frustrated, but all the while the people are rushing around him, Lars sees Herdis' number in large print everywhere.

"How can I wait two weeks to call her? What if the number is one digit off?" he worries.

He tries to calm himself. He reasons that if he has the wrong number, he can run random number scans until he hits the correct phone number. After all, the government is paying the phone bill. The security issue might be another problem, but he is bound and determined to find her again. His life has certainly changed in the last few weeks, and he was a little surprised that he couldn't escape the strong emotions he got from such an irrational sequence of events. There was no denying it, however; however illogical, that the emotions are real and here to stay. He wishes he could spend more time daydreaming about Herdis. But it seems that every time he begins to go over her phone number or the excitement of calling her, there is an issue in the facility and he needs to go back to work. This began to anger Lars. The government control on the project is becoming so ridiculous that Lars begins to wonder exactly how long he could take it. He is constantly frustrated by government motivations. Sure, government and science have been at odds for all of history, but when the military sees the hope of a new weapon or other means of gaining an advantage over a real or imagined adversary, it pushes science and scientist with a speed that makes them dizzy. Lars still has difficulty thinking of the Manhattan Project, the atomic bomb that killed several hundred thousand Japanese. True, the history of the relationship between science and military would fill volumes. It has not always been a harmonious relationship, but some of greatest leaps forward have been motivated by the search for greater weaponry and killing power. Remembering this, Lars vows to let the truth be told and to not be undermined by government interest.

"The true story will be told, and history will not repeat itself, at least not in my lab," he thinks.

But Lars has a grand battle before him. He decides to gather his fellow researchers for a meeting because something must be done to protect the scientific integrity of the messenger. He and the other scientists already know that they are not really in control of the study. The military, hoping for a new weapon and a new computer technology, is firmly in control. They continually attempt to intimidate Lars and the other scientists. As the other scientists gather for Lars' clandestine meeting, one of the scientists passes a note that states he has discovered bugs, and not the crawling type, in his room and on his phones. The scientists quickly realize the danger and decide to avoid discussing anything significant where they can be heard. Through quiet meetings and secret messages, they agree on a plan to pretend that the project is going far slower than it really is, and they devise a coded system by which they can record all of the output from the messenger, and it will be of no value to anyone without the decoder. This must be done, for they all agree that the message MUST be heard and available to the world. Specially encrypted tapes are stashed away from prying government eyes for review later. As Lars is wrapping up one of these secret meetings with a fellow scientist, he hears a very loud noise coming from outside. The scientists separate, and Lars races toward the outdoors and to the gates. There, he sees a group of radical theists screaming and protesting. Lars now knows his problems have just gotten bigger. A much more formidable foe of science has arisen to shut down the study. The old nemesis of intelligent and objective thinking has been awakened.

Lars has long known that the oldest and one of the most formidable foes of science has always been religion and its leadership. It was the religious leaders that put Galileo under arrest and made Copernicus recount his well-documented theory that the earth traveled around the sun instead of the Christian-approved thesis that the earth was the center of things and God had created heaven and earth as man's dominion. Religion is blind, and the facts, no matter how clear and how unmistakable, were never given a second look. Certainly, when the Dead Sea Scrolls were discovered by a Bedouin shepherd in the Judean desert in 1947, the religious community was terrified that the Bible as we know it would be refuted or changed, putting into question their mythology. The researchers of the Scrolls had a monumental project to put the pieces and fragments together and learn of the Qumran community, the Essenes, and their writings. We now have another view of the world just before the birth of Jesus. Some of the Bible is confirmed and some refuted, but that is only because, as the years went on, it was written and rewritten by authors with differing goals.

As Lars stands outside those gates and thought of all the historical religious impediments to scientific study, his heart sinks. Here he is, trying to help humanity find the answers, and he is being fought by those he wishes to help. As he stands there, he listened to the religious leaders, mainly of the more radical Christian and Muslim faiths, stand before the protesters and preach about how the "devil thing" must be destroyed before any further work can be done. They call the messenger the devil's doing and plead for its destruction by a nuclear detonation, so no evil evidence could possibly remain. It seems so irrational to need a nuclear weapon to destroy such a small and magnificently designed device, but when you have God on your side, reason is lost.

Standing there, amidst the preaching and the screams of agreement from the protesters, Lars knows similar scenes were taking place around the world. Preachers were standing in their pulpits, telling their congregations to write their legislators, participate in demonstrations, and use violence if necessary to prevent the "Devil" from sweeping through the world. Why must it turn to this?

Unfortunately, Lars knew the answer only too well. If communication actually came from another earth time or worse from "out there," it would again place religions mythologies at risk and they may lose constituents and the bottom line, revenue. Religious leaders, just as they have always done, oppose any progress and are afraid that a real truth may be revealed and shatter their mythology. This would be a big blow to organized religion. Who would need them? The truth has always scared the hell out of religions, and they have always reacted to stifle free inquiry and investigation.

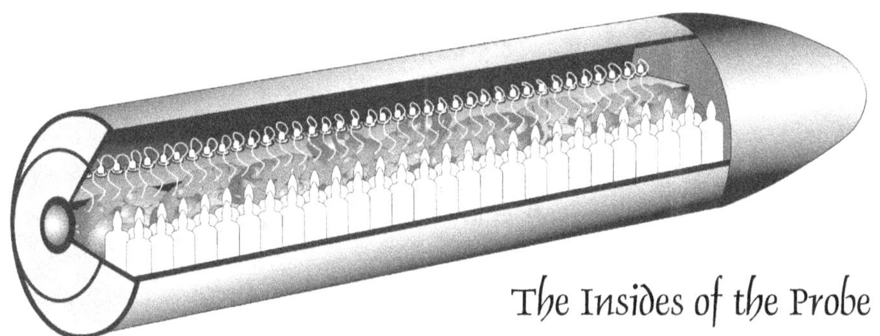

The Insides of the Probe

So not only do the scientists need to protect themselves from their keepers but also from the radical faithful at the gates. The theists are terrified that an authoritative statement from an alien intelligence would destroy their mythology in one fell swoop. As Lars looks at the mass pressing up against the gates, he wonders if these ancient enemies of science will again interfere in some way with logical advance of knowledge. Contemplating this, Lars begins to walk back toward the facility. The door opens before he arrives, and Josh shouts to him that the tool has arrived. Anxious and excited, Lars runs inside. The big moment has arrived, and the team is ready to open the shell.

Scientists, military, and administrators alike all group around the lab, nervously waiting as Lars uses the tool to remove the end cap of the missile very, very carefully. As he pulls the cap away, things are revealed that no human has ever seen before or even imagined. Tiny filaments connect strange little parts, some connecting to a Plutonium nuclear powered battery that resembles those used in our space probes. The scientists recognize the battery, but the rest is completely foreign. None of the super scientists can even suggest where to start, gazing at the collection of filaments and small ampoules. The contemplative silence is suddenly broken by an over-eager guard named Ellen who suggests that it resembles a brain, a sort of living organism, like a flying brain. Lars thinks that the guard may be right. He proceeds carefully, removing the contents from the hard-shell encasing. A row of fifty-four ampoules is visible, nestled in a protected containment. As the scientists look on, all realize that this maze of filaments is going to present a major problem for the computer scientists to understand. There seems to be no instruction book and the scientists wonder how they are supposed to use this thing. But Lars is certain that there must be a plan provided by the sender. But how to find it?

Lars and the other scientists carefully film and document all phases of the opening. During the process, the filaments are determined to be connections, like the wiring of an organic computer, a heuristic (trained to learn for yourself) living device. Humans dreamed of such systems but so far lacked the technology to build one. The obvious advantage to this kind of system is its ability to be self-learning and self-organizing - a computer that can adapt and grow and "think" like the human brain! The scientists buzz around the computer like children with a new toy. If the scientists can understand it and if they can get it to work, it will greatly assist current development efforts. But the questions remain. What are these sealed ampoules? Where do they go? How does it work? These questions swim through Lars' head as he examines the device. He observes what appears to be some ciphers on each ampoule. In fact, twenty-six of them appear to be pairs with the same markings, save for two with different markings. Lars wonders if these two may be an instruction manual of some kind. Much study must be done before the scientists attempt to open any of the ampoules, but there is no doubt that these ampoules possess the information being preserved for a yet undefined purpose.

Lars assembles a computer science team to attack these problems.

"Go slowly and do not disturb anything until we fully understand its purpose," Lars orders.

Lars feels strongly that this is a message or messenger from another intelligent civilization, maybe extraterrestrial or maybe from a past earth civilization, lost for hundreds or thousands of years but anxious to leave a record. Lars wonders if the messenger will reveal some truth in all the myths and fables of ancient societies, perhaps even throwing doubts on some of the theories of the archaeological and paleontological sciences. Lars knows this was a monumental find, but he still struggles to solve its mysteries. He is sure the makers wanted their story told, and he is sure they provided instructions on using their messenger, but Lars just wasn't sure exactly how or where he could find these very important instructions. Would he even understand them?

Lars thoughts are suddenly interrupted. He hears another loud noise coming from near the gates. The team rushes out to see about the commotion. A large contingent of the faithful has set up camp at the gates to the facility, and the protest seems to have taken a violent turn. "Typical", thinks Lars, knowing similar scenes are occurring all over the country as the fear of the unknown mounts. Lars knows that incidents like these could jeopardize the entire project. He quickly turns to his team and orders them back to the project. The world is holding its breath as it waits for the translation from "the messenger", and Lars is intent on making that message heard. Before joining the others, he makes his way to the crowd and makes an announcement to the press. He assures the press repeatedly that his team is a long way from any decoding and that it could, in fact, take years before the message is revealed. Knowing his statement will delay the panic and appease the masses for awhile, Lars hurries back to the complex where he knows his capable team will uncover the message much sooner than he let on. After all, the senders of this message were intent on having it read and understood. Lars has no doubt that the senders would make the message as simple, logical, and straight forward as possible. Still, the equipment they sent is most unusual, a brain and some DNA in vials. Lars does know one thing for sure; he and his team will have to change their whole way of thinking about information storage to understand this device and its hidden purpose.

As the days wear on, more and more specialists are brought in, including a brain surgeon, DNA experts, and organic computer specialists to help figure out the organic circuitry. They now, in a relatively short time, know more about the workings of this strange brain than we knew after centuries of study of the human brain. As Lars looks at the progress, he can't help but wonder why research is only supported when there is a compelling national need. He knows the answer; he simply hates to admit it. There are only two things, greed and fear, that motivated scientific endeavors. The curiosity, the very stuff of which science should be made, has long ago been lost. But Lars still has it. He turns his attention again to the object which fills him with such anticipation and joy.

"Now where is the read out?" one scientist asks.

"Where do we hook up to the little fellow and get an output?" inquires another.

People start bustling about as the awakening of the messenger seems to draw nearer. The scientists find a sort of receptacle, which is elongated and is the terminal of numerous nerve endings. Upon further inspection, they reason that this is the output connector and that each nerve ending is a terminal with a fluorescent tip emitting a pulse of light when activated. At least, this is the current theory as no pulses are presently visible. The scientists quickly realize that they must manufacture yet another tool - this time one capable of making a connection between the complex miniature connections with a suitable array of photodiodes and the computer systems. A design is worked out and a microcircuit on a silicon wafer probe is fabricated. Micrometer adjustments are provided to make small physical adjustments if necessary. With the new tool in hand, the scientists remain unsure of the form or voltage or light intensity or wavelength of any output signal that this new connector will provide. Still, Lars feels that the designers wanted the finders to be able to read their message and would try to make it fool proof. "And damn fool proof at that," he thinks. They may even have sent us a brain because they knew we would understand that type of design. Lars grows increasingly anxious to unlock the mystery, but the big event is delayed again.

After much debate, Monday is set as test day. The vial with the strange character markings will be opened first. The scientists concur that this vial contains the instructions, the on-off switch, the help disk, and the initializing disk. With careful hands, the scientists begin the test by dropping a portion of the precious fluid into the receptacle which at this point, resembled a worm's mouth. The output connector, if that is what it is, is connected to a vast array of computer equipment. Once the team gets a signal, if they get a signal, the cryptographers can go to work to try to understand the message. The drops are inputted, and nothing happens. Questions buzz.

"Is the temperature right?"

"Is there something else we should be doing?"

"Should we just wait? After all, this little fellow has been here for several hundred thousand years, waiting. Let's give it a chance."

Everyone holds their breath. There are some fluctuations at the output but nothing recognizable. Then, it comes in a flood of information, an endless stream of binary codes. Once the electrodes are adjusted properly and the system compensates for the proper voltage swings, the message comes through loud and clear. It appears to be better at longer wavelengths in the red and infrared. The scientists quickly realize that new equipment needs to be designed and ordered to decode this message. The test is put on hold, and the equipment is set to arrive by special delivery the following day.

But the next day, as the new and very essential equipment arrives at the gates, a swarm of protesters seize the van and hold the driver hostage. They demand television coverage and broadcast their desire for the destruction of the messenger and the cessation of all work on the devil's thing. Lars hears the commotion as he pours over yesterday's data and fears the worst. He runs to the gates to find the van, the angry mob, and the guards all engaged in a very volatile situation. A security officer pulls Lars aside and insists he not panic; apparently the SWAT team is on its way. This does nothing to calm Lars but rather incites him.

"They are going to shoot these people," Lars thinks. "They may be misled, but they are good, well-meaning people expressing their beliefs the best way they know how."

Lars desperately tries to make his way to the microphone; he surely must be able to help the people understand. He fights hard to get to the podium, while the fear he has for the van's driver grows and the security surrounds him. He hopes that hearing words from a scientist may appease the masses, and the impending police confrontation can be avoided. He finally makes his way to the microphone and pleads with the protesters to release the van driver and hear him out. He asks for a representative from the group to open up a discussion but no one steps forward. Without a moment more of wait, he starts forward toward the group, determined that only his immediate action can cause a peaceful turn of events. If someone does not do something, someone is going to get hurt. The police quickly try to interfere, but he waves them off and orders them to move back to a safer distance. The police surprisingly obey his command, and Lars is surprised he can continue. As he struggles through the crowd, he focuses on reaching the van. He needs to rescue the driver and his equipment. The crowd certainly does not realize how important the van is to the project. In the back of his mind, Lars hopes that the crowd will be able to understand the importance of the project and the benefits of his team's study.

As Lars approaches the van, a young woman presses through the crowd of protesters and meets him face to face. Lars stops dead in his tracks. It is the mystery girl he has been dreaming about. He can't believe this is happening. As Herdis approaches, the security guards grab her, but Lars shoves them off and orders them to back off. As Lars and Herdis meet there in the street, they both take a step back. He is speechless and has no idea what to say, and he rarely finds himself without words. Seeing his struggle, Herdis meets his eyes and smiles gently.

"When I saw you, the same person I ran with, I had to come forward. I know you are no monster out to undue God's work."

As she says this, she realizes that her attraction for him has grown, as has his for her.

"We are not monsters. We are only interested in truth. Can that be bad?" he softly speaks to her.

He gently grabs her hand and makes his way back to the microphone where he offers to take Herdis and two others on a tour of the laboratory to see for themselves what is happening inside. Certainly, this is an offer that even the most zealous could not refuse. There is silence as Herdis returns to the protesters and convinces them the offer is for real and not some sort of artificial attempt at appeasing the crowd. The group agrees, much to Lars' relief, to release the driver and to have representatives tour the facility. Herdis brings the two other volunteers forward to meet Lars. One is a minister named Ronald, and the other is a creationist scientist with a PhD from a religious school in California with no scientific credibility. Upon the introduction, Lars quickly realizes that this is the only way to save his probe and feels his interruption at least helped to save the life of the driver.

As Lars and his companions make a start toward the facility, the guards and the police object vehemently. But, since it was Lars' actions that abated the conflict, the agents and police have been following his orders. He finds himself a little surprised and pleased with his new power. He tells the security force to escort the group for the tour and that he will be responsible.

He thinks to himself, "Responsible to whom?"

As the security force surrounds the new visitors, Lars has no time to speak to Herdis, but he is very glad she is here. He watches her as the group makes its way down to the home of "the messenger." Lars steps forward, feeling a need to prepare the group a little before the group sees the missile. He addresses the group, explaining that the capsule is neither God nor Devil but sent by intelligent people just like them.

"We do not know what it says, but we do know it was left to tell their story. It is just a machine, like a movie, which I guess may be a sort of history book. Maybe we all can learn from them. Maybe they are warning us of future catastrophes which we can avoid. Please do not judge the little fellow until we have heard what it has to say."

The group is listening intently, and Lars is a bit surprised to find the religious zealots considering what he has to say. He wonders if they are truly the enemies he imagined. He is encouraged by their attention and decides it is time to continue the tour. He shows the facilities and explains some of the scientific methods in use. Finally, the group catches sight of the "devil." He shows the observers how the feared object is just a little shell with a very sophisticated organic computer brain, which he hopes to communicate with. It is no miracle or supernatural thing; it is just a piece of technology like a television, cell phone, or computer.

The group studies the little fellow for a very long time. They are impressed with the whole facility, the find, and most of all, the sincerity of Lars and his words. Lars senses that he has successfully communicated with the group and suggests they enter his office for a deeper discussion.

"Ignorance is both of our worst enemies," he starts.

The group nods in agreement and Lars continues on, expressing his gratitude for their attitudes and involvement. He then makes a most unusual suggestion. He offers to include them in his team and allow them access each day to view and monitor progress, give input, and basically be a part of the project. While he is stating this, for the reasons of the good of the discovery, he can't help but get excited at the prospect of having Herdis nearby him for such a long period of time. He regains his thoughts and continues to try to ease the team into the idea.

"It is not against God or anything. It is only a search for the TRUTH," he concludes.

The group discusses what they have seen and agree that they are quite impressed with Lars and appreciate his frank and professional manner. As they start the return to their fellow protesters outside, Lars attempts to get a word in with Herdis but finds it difficult. He knows he must instead focus on getting back to the chaos before something tragic and unnecessary happens. Lars never revealed how badly the equipment in the van is needed and desperately hopes it has been spared as he hurries toward the gate.

At the gate, the group disperses, and Lars waits anxiously for the word on the van. Soon, Ronald the minister, returns with a suggestion that they set up a TV link whereby the entire group can see what he had seen on the tour. He also suggests that some type of facility could be erected near the gate for the members of the protest group to live in while this extraordinary event takes place. Lars is concerned, however, that too much access could sabotage the mission. He is a believer; however, in opening the doors of communication and knowledge and the housing could help him achieve these goals. In fact, he thought, he ought to house the press as well, who are now frantic to get an equal tour. What better way to spread the knowledge and wipe away ignorance! Lars quickly lets go of his concern about too much access, partly because of his belief in communication and partly because he can see the van is still surrounded. He agrees to Ronald's suggestion, and the van is released.

As Lars watches the van drive off toward the facility, he stops and thinks about how life has changed for him yet again. Here he is, a scientist, with his life all organized and logical, now finding himself, in one short month, head of the greatest scientific adventure ever, in love with a protester he doesn't even really know, and partners with a minister and a creation scientist!! But there is no time to dwell on the irony. Lars finally has the parts he needs to retest the machine.

Lars reenters the world of the facility where people are excitedly rushing about preparing for the new test. A preliminary study of the ampoules indicates that they contain an organic fluid. The filamentary maze is extremely complicated and takes a while to trace out to a point where they know what to expect. As he pinpoints the correct location, Lars is bursting with excitement. He can hardly believe that the dream he has had all his life of a documented, real encounter with a past or alien intelligence may be happening! With trembling hands, he inspects the many inscriptions on the inside of the device. He gives the inscriptions to the cryptographers who study these intently, knowing that every second they take to decipher it is holding up what may well be the most significant discovery in the history of man. After some agonizing work, they discover a basis for the language and find that the two extra ampoules are the instruction books for the device. The scientists carefully remove the ampoules, taking special care in a double-sealed containment chamber many feet underground as a precaution against any strange viruses or radioactive contaminants that might escape into Earth's atmosphere. After this step is complete, the scientists begin to try to decipher the emissions still coming from the messenger. There seems to be considerable redundancy in the signal, which would be expected in trying to communicate with another intelligence that may not be familiar with your techniques. It is determined that the first vial is the on-off switch, the initializing program, and may include instructions or a help file. The remainder of the vials contain the message. All are very anxious to get on to the next step of adding more vials and getting the message.

Outside the laboratory, the protesters and media are watching every step of this historic event on a series of big-screen televisions at the gates, just as Lars had promised. They actually seem satisfied and glad, in a way, to be a part of things. Interest is high, and fear is reduced. Knowledge is power.

CHAPTER IV (VENUS)

The Trial

Jonic's eyes meet Nadia's. He sees the tears but cannot think of any words of comfort. They sit in silence around their kitchen table for hours, neither one able to accept the fact they both know. How they wish that they had never allowed Kylia to play that day on the bouncing device. He had fallen and seriously hit his head, resulting in multiple brain contusions. At first, it did not seem too serious, but gradually, he lost the use of his members, and his powers of memory and reason began to diminish. Jonic and Nadia spent countless hours waiting for tests to be run by the medical staff and waited to hear Kylia's fate. Finally, they received the news that the medical staff could not operate or correct the situation. Their hearts sank, and they have been sitting here in silence ever since they heard the news. Jonic and Nadia know that if a member of the community is incapacitated or even diminished in performance, he or she is considered for banishment to the surface, which, of course, is a death sentence. Jonic wonders how his community got to this awful state, but deep inside he knows. It all seemed so logical before it became so personal.

Jonic has long hated the population control laws, but he has a rational mind and saw their purpose. Under the new laws, when a permitted child is born, a "designate," perhaps the oldest in the community, is sent to the surface. Jonic knew this was harsh, but necessary. Venusian society realizes the need for the young, and since the carrying capacity of the underground communities is limited, someone must always go to the surface to make room for new life. The population laws are so strictly enforced that families are banished for births without permits, and some families even resort to paying assassins for some "midnight limiting" so that older family members may remain a while longer. Jonic has never understood the desperation of these families, until today. He had never had to banish someone close to him, either for age or for breaking a law. Banishment to the surface is the most common punishment for breaking laws, as it accomplishes two goals: it is a severe punishment, death, and it reduces the population temporarily. Down here, if you are not an active, necessary part of the community, you are eliminated.

There are not even any retirees; everyone must be productive until banishment. There is no room for the sick, infirmed, handicapped, or incapable. Even anyone with a self-inflicted wound or health diminishment is considered for elimination. For example, anyone overweight according to the minimum body mass index is warned and then considered for banishment. Any drug use, which has harmful health effects, also receives a visit from the government. It is the obligation of each citizen to be in as healthy a condition as possible in order not to be a burden to the community. Everyone tries very hard to be a contributing member and a functioning part of society for it is a matter of survival. On top of this, the residents of Venus are always being tested to prove their worth. The government holds continual "games" to test the society members and keeps records on their condition.

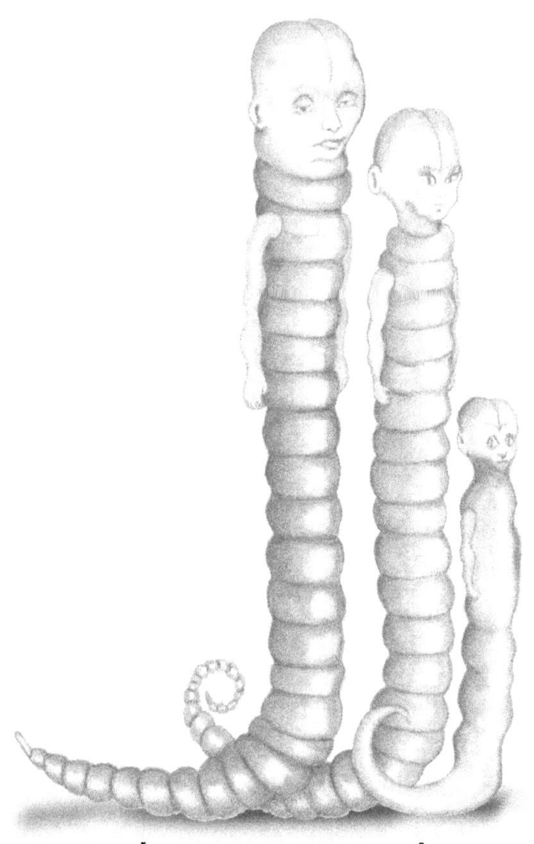

The Venusian Family

Those that prove unfit to contribute to the society are considered for elimination. Room is limited and only the strong are permitted to stay. Jonic had never given too much thought to the process. He possesses badly needed skills, and so he is an exception to these general rules. But Jonic knows his child does not enjoy the same immunity as him.

As Jonic gazes again at his wife across the table, he reaches for her hand. There must be some way out of this. He thinks about the government and how it was designed. Could he find a legal loophole? Could he blackmail the government? He tries desperately to think of a way to spare his child. But Jonic knows the Venusian government was designed to be foolproof. They had learned a lot from the former civilization, and he knew the new government had been carefully thought out and was probably impenetrable.

Like other Venusian communities, Jonic's community is governed by a collective that actually, so far, has worked. All leaders must pass a rigorous system of testing, including brain scans and analysis, to find leaders who are selfless, loving, dedicated individuals. From childhood, everyone is retested annually for leadership potential, physical fitness, and achievement skills. And since those seriously lacking are considered for banishment, there is a great incentive to learn and become a serious part of a productive community. This is in contrast to the surface philosophy where the young were never sure of their goals and boredom, drugs, and lack of interest in education ran rampant.

Jonic admittedly finds the new system much more appealing, but the harshness of the laws to insure underground survival is difficult to accept. But deep inside, Jonic knows he'd never trade it for the world of the surface. On the surface, leaders achieved their roles by family position, money, and power. It was those leaders whose greed caused this terrible situation. If Venusians had only instituted this method of leader selection while living on the surface, they would still be there, living happily in the open spaces instead of facing certain termination as a species. But during the surface days, the primary decisions were made by "leaders", mostly self-appointed and selected by power, corruption, influence, and religion. This was dominance in action. So while life was relatively good on the surface, the leader-selection system of self-appointment was basically tolerated. Assassination was a method of replacement; leaders were appointed over the popular vote by manipulation of the courts, and dictators seized power through control of the corrupt police or army. Now, in the caves facing extinction, it was far too late for the people to decide to take the responsibility of running their own affairs. Today, greed and power are less important and survival is paramount. Now, the decisions of life and death are made daily, by everyone and, right or wrong, all have a hand in it.

Under these extreme conditions, the Venusians were able to establish a working democracy. In the new government, each unit votes for a representative who meets weekly at a forum which is open to all but only the representative can speak. Each home has a monitor and a vote box, and everyone votes on every issue. Since lives are so frequently at stake, the votes are carefully cast, and the population stays well-informed. Everyone feels he or she truly has a voice in the operation of the community because each person votes each day on the issues before him or her. This requires a great deal of personal effort from each member of the community to investigate and decide the issues of the day. In hindsight, it is obvious that, while on the surface, the government functioned basically by default because the people were too lazy to direct the goals of their leaders. So the leaders directed the affairs of state to their own personal best interests. This resulted in the eventual total destruction of the surface world. Since that time, the community has been forged into a close functioning unit and the people devote enormous time and study to the past, and what caused such a catastrophe to occur.

In the distant past of surface life there were a number of inspired spiritual leaders who tried to turn the leadership role toward the good, but, in each case, the establishment of officials, priests, and the powerful subverted the movements toward dominance. There was one teacher who taught that the traditional religious covenants with God be supplanted by a new covenant " love your enemy". This teaching espoused a direct connection of the individual with his God without the trappings of dogma, ritual, and a priestly clergy. This teacher claimed to be sent by the ONE to free the people from guilt and religions and connect them directly with the ONE. This philosophy spread like magic through out the land, but, as the popularity grew the establishment had the teacher executed and prostituted his message by again inserting the priestly cast in between God, the ONE, and the people. The message was rewritten to empower the powerful, and, now, Government had God on its side. Dominance was reestablished.

Certainly, the Venusians learned a very hard lesson. Jonic knows that the laws and procedures in place insure the survival of the community. And he never had any problem with this somewhat militaristic state before. But now that his own child may be subject to termination, Jonic feels trapped and alone. Sure, this system is far better than the surface government, but why must he lose his child? Jonic hates himself for being so selfish. He has already enjoyed many more privileges than his fellow Venusians. Since he is a respected and needed scientist and since he and Nadia scored very high on the "Desirable Breeding Scale", he was given the privilege of having a child. Sure, it is a far cry from the free and open surface days when anyone could breed with anyone he or she chose and produce as many children as they pleased. In fact, during the surface days, abortion of a conceived fetus was discouraged and even illegal in some locals. The religions promoted large families in a breeding race to try and out produce other factions. To accomplish this, they enlisted their perpetual ally, the government, which also desired rapid growth in order to provide soldiers and an ever-expanding consumer market. But now, in the confined spaces of the underground life, this luxury is no longer afforded. Jonic knows he should feel very lucky to have been awarded such a privilege in a land where the rights to reproduce are so restricted. But no matter how hard he tries, Jonic only feels like the unluckiest man in the world.

Tightening his grip on Nadia's hand, he knows that they must leave their sadness behind and try to prepare for the trial. A special panel or court makes banishment decisions, with the affirmation of the community by an evening vote. There are many rules and much legal maneuvering. The accused have rights and are entitled to be heard and present witnesses and arguments. Nadia knows a trial is bound to ensue and sees the resolve in Jonic's eyes and nods her head. They must compose themselves to fight this battle. If Kylia's condition worsens, which it is expected to, a trial will become the order of the day. Jonic and Nadia's only hope is to somehow make the case that this whole situation is not the fault of his offspring but the fault of the community as a whole for not taking a more assertive role during the later surface days. He and Nadia spend hours over the course of the next few days methodically delving through the files of trials and history to put together a case to save their only offspring.

The fateful day finally arrives, and the government notifies Jonic of its intent to consider the case of his son as being no longer a potential contributor to the community. The first hearing is scheduled to occur in approximately two weeks. Jonic and Nadia are frantic. They work night and day, studying every angle. Meanwhile, they notice that Kylia's mental abilities diminish daily. The doctor's reports are not encouraging, and a cloud of fear and doubt begins to engulf Jonic and Nadia as they try to avoid the inevitable.

The hearing date arrives quickly, too quickly for Kylia's distraught family. As Jonic sits in the courtroom, questions pound through his head. Who is to blame for the terrible situation we are in? Who is responsible for my son being tried? But Jonic knows the answer, and he knows his attempts at assigning blame will do him no good. He is so angry, but there is nothing he can do. Instead, he resolves to focus on the huge task before him and concentrate on his defense. The judge nods to him, and Jonic walks to the front of the room.

Jonic begins by laying out his case based on the argument that the offspring of those that destroyed their surface life should be banished first to keep the population balance. It had long been established that the descendants of the destroyers would be penalized. He outlined for his audience the certain individuals and groups singled out for blame in the surface trials held right before they entered their dark world and the new government was established. The groups that were decided to be culpable were the corporate executives, lawyers, politicians, and religious leaders for the following reasons:

Corporate Executives: They misled the public with their money and power to reject alternate power sources. They funded the anti-nuclear campaign and created false and misleading propaganda denigrating the desirability of alternative power. In addition, they made huge donations to be sure their candidates were elected even when they knew that global warming was a reality. They funded research aimed to confuse the public and to sidetrack the results of honest scientific endeavor.

Lawyers: They have been blight on society since their inception. They have made a mockery of justice and fair dealing. The law should be fair for all and understood by all. There are no lawyers in the underground society. The lawyer's crime was that they added and abetted to insiders to pervert the courts and mislead the public.

Politicians: They may be the worst of all, as they took the money from the corporations and intentionally misled the population to assist the energy industry. If they told the truth they would not be elected.

Religious Leaders: They led their flock to obey the government, all in the name of God and country.

After the reminder to the courtroom of the culpable parties, Jonic goes on to list the descendants of the original convicted transgressors, which number fifteen local people currently living in the community. "Why haven't these people been eliminated as decided during the surface trials? Why must my son, a descendant of the scientists who argued, lobbied, and fought the establishment to stop burning fossil fuels be banished before these people?" He pleads with the court to banish one of the fifteen descendants of the greedy surface dwellers in lieu of his son. To emphasize his point, Jonic revisits the sore subject of life on the surface. He reminds his listeners how people did not pay attention to the warnings of the scientists who correctly predicted the catastrophic climate changes that were about to befall the planet. He reminds them how the government of the planet consisted of an elite class who, by heredity, limited top education and governmental advancement to a select few. Jonic continues on.

"These elite received a superior education, belonged to proper social groups, and basically, inherited the leadership role. The members of this group guarded their monopoly powers assiduously and sometimes violently. Their wealth and power is derived from the ownership, control, and distribution of the energy sources. Fossil fuel supplies were plentiful and provided the perfect source for the powers at be to maintain a tight grip on the status quo. There were many superior power sources at the time, such as nuclear power, but these are not as accessible to the power elite. They encourage and fund environmental groups such as Friends of Venus and Save Our Planet to protest against and lobby against nuclear power generation. The voice of the scientists was drowned out by these well-meaning but technologically ignorant groups! "Don't you remember? Am I not speaking the truth?"

Jonic looks at his audience and tries to read their faces. He sees the anger, the sadness, and the fear on their faces. No one wants to talk about this, and Jonic feels a little chagrin for having to bring such pain back into their minds. But the life of the son is on the line, and he has to do all he can to help him. He takes a deep breath and starts again.

"The result, as you know, was the ever-increasing use of fossil fuels and the inescapable "Green House Warming." It all started slowly so no one noticed, except a few who were in the path of the floods and storms. Actually, the weather in the temperate zones improved and the warmer climate was actually welcomed. But as the scientists tried to explain, the traps or sinks for the excess carbon dioxide, the principal green house gas, were filling up and when full their effectiveness greatly diminished; the results were a rapid carbon dioxide build up, raising temperatures. And, as you know, all of this was irreversible in a reasonable time period and that is why we are now down here instead of up there in the light.

The words choke Jonic for a moment, and he pauses to look at Nadia. She nods to him, encouraging him to continue. The story is hard to tell; the emotions are difficult, but they both know it is their only hope of saving their son. With a heavy heart and the words almost impossible, Jonic presses on.

"I need not remind you how this group of greedy, ruthless politicians was aided by the old coalition of religions. These religions preached conformance to government policies in exchange for the government providing the religions a license, access to schools to inculcate the young, and, in some cases, a denominational monopoly in the society. The government maintained tax-free churches; donors could avoid taxes through gifts; and religious schools were subsidized by government funding. Certainly, you can all see who is to blame for the ruin of our world. It is neither my son nor the forefathers of my family. Why must you punish the very people trying to save the world over the descendants of those who destroyed it?

Jonic's last question leaves his eyes full of tears, but he knows his final statement remains. In all his life, Jonic has never had to do anything so difficult. He searches the crowd for signs of compassion. He can't be sure if he sees any, but he hopes desperately to change their minds. How can he live without his son? How will he ever recover? In desperation, he continues on.

"This potent combination of corruption, greed, and complacency enabled an over-burning of fossil fuels that put too much carbon dioxide back into the atmosphere. The effect accelerated rapidly. And as the threat became imminent, the government leaders were arrested, and the energy production was shifted to nuclear. We sent probes to nearby planets such as Earth, and plans were made to start digging into the ground and to stockpile parts and materials. We designed and built huge underground nuclear power plants designed to run for a very long time. Cooling systems were installed. But all this was too little too late as the surface became hotter and hotter. There was no escape from the world that these power-hungry individuals created. And now, we are trapped in hell because they wanted bigger bank accounts. You know the story. You know the history. I am not telling you anything you do not know, but am I telling you something you have put out of your mind? Have you forgotten the joy that was taken from us? Why weren't the offspring of those responsible banished immediately? Why do some of these descendants live among us now? The progeny of the accursed should be banished, not my innocent son. We've argued over this issue a long time, and each time we've voted, it has been a very close race, so I know many of you here today agree with me. The DNA of everyone is catalogued; we know who the offspring of the "accursed ones" are. Shouldn't they be rounded up and made to pay for their forefathers transgressions? This is really the case before the court. Who do you want punished for your dark existence, my son or the people that caused your fate?"

With these final words, Jonic returns to his seat. He holds Nadia tightly as his heart beats rapidly. The court deliberates, and Jonic is unsure if he will survive the next few minutes. Finally, the court reaches a decision. It is banishment for Kylia. Jonic stands up, half in shock but enraged with anger. He screams at the courtroom. He warns the court that perhaps their cooling system will stop working if his son is killed. He is desperate and he is not sure that he doesn't have it in him to destroy the underground world. His threats are mistaken for the emotional ravings of a parent about to lose his child. The decision remains. Kylia will be banished, no exceptions. This decision must be confirmed by the voters that night but an affirmative vote is expected.

As Nadia and Jonic make their way out of the courtroom, Jonic's mood changes. His rage has turned to conviction. He waits for the vote, which is announced quickly. Nadia watches Jonic numbly make his way toward the central cooling control room, and she knows what he is leaving there. Inside the cooling room, he places a home-made bomb and then returns home. As Jonic arrives at his house, he is greeted by silence. Jonic locks the door, gathers his wife and child in his arms, and waits.

The end comes quickly.

CHAPTER V (EARTH)

The Message

As Lars finishes his log for the day and checks the circuits to the multimedia display for the protesters outside, he realizes he can barely think. His body feels so tired and his mind preoccupied, not only with the study but the thoughts of a beautiful woman. He quickly resolves to go for a run, and knowing Herdis has a passion for the same, he straightens up his clothes and heads for the gates. After dodging several questions from the demonstrators, Lars finally finds Herdis. She is standing alone, seemingly mesmerized by the monitors, and Lars senses that she feels overwhelmed by the incidents of the day. As he approaches her, he can't help but see the look in her eyes that tells of her confusion. When she declines his offer to go for a run, Lars is not too surprised. He is concerned about her but knows he can't push. She is going through a difficult time, and Lars resolves to run alone this time. As he walks away, Herdis almost calls him back but restrains. Her faith has been shaken by this handsome scientist who makes so much sense and yet seems quite dangerous. Herdis is sure she has never felt so torn. Her life had, up until now, been so clear and comfortable. Desiring distraction, she decides she cannot watch Lars any longer and turns to focus on the monitors once again.

Lars is filled with disappointment as he heads out for his run, but he understands how Herdis must be feeling. He longs to be near her, to help her through her struggle, but he knows that she needs time to sort out her thoughts. As he strides along the desert trails, Lars begins to feel more uplifted. His thoughts wander to the project and he realizes how much he has grown into his leadership position. It feels as if he is much more in control now, and he senses that the others recognize that he is truly the one in charge. This comforts Lars, in the face of the stifling security and the fear of the government hurting the integrity of the project. Lars is sure he has the trust of his team and he knows he can lead them to a great discovery, but he also knows how powerful the government can be. As he glides through the Nevada desert, Lars begins to devise a plan to keep ahead of his keepers. He finishes his run excitedly, calling Josh Van Dever into his office the second he returns.

Josh is just finishing up with some final inspections when he gets Lars' call. Josh has a feeling that Lars has some sort of plan to protect the messenger. They are both well aware that the team is just reaching the moment where contact could be possible; the excitement can be felt all around the compound. To contact a yet unknown source of knowledge at least equal to ours in technology is the dream of every adventurer. But the closer they get, the more dangerous it becomes; the knowledge could be lost in a battle for military technology. With this in mind and still angry about how rudely they took the rights to his discovery away, Josh hurries to Lars' office to hopefully work on a plan to preserve the truth. As Josh enters the room, he finds Lars pacing back and forth in his running shorts. Josh smiles to himself, knowing that Lars does his best thinking while on a run and knows Lars must be beside himself to call him in before he even showers. Lars beckons Josh to follow him, and Josh nods compliantly, knowing they are going out of reach of government ears. When all is secure, Lars begins the meeting.

"I've been thinking. You and I both know how close we are. Do you think we can place a time delay and a deleting program between what is learned and what we allow the overseers to know without detection?" "It will be difficult, but it may be the only way to be sure the message will ever get out to the people for whom it was intended."

"Precisely."

With that, the two scientists begin their plans to secretly build a delay factor into the translation program. They work quickly, knowing that without protection, "they," the government and the theists, could "reinterpret" the message any way they like. All the counter security has been slowing down the scientific work but Lars, Josh, and the entire scientific team feel it is imperative that the true story be preserved. Since the actual progress is much better than originally anticipated, these security measures are certainly worth the risk. The team, well attuned to the security monitoring them, manages to install the delay system and breathes a sigh of relief, knowing they may have just preserved the truth.

Feeling more secure, the team is now finally comfortable to move forward. The key to the problem, of course, is how to establish and hook up to the device. It is obvious to all the scientists that the senders intended to have the finders be able to communicate with it. But how? For the first step, the scientists request permission to move their study to a remote-controlled clean room so as not to contaminate the fluid in the vials, and more importantly, not to release some toxin or viruses on the Earth. Of course, these are the reasons given for the move, but the truth is that the new environment allowed the scientists to more closely cover up their progress.

The scientists work around the clock on the messenger. On their faces, the wear is evident from the lack of sleep and the tedious trial and error process. The last disappointment for the team came from inserting the two vials. There was some initial excitement by a signal output, but it turned out to be simply a carrier wave, with no information that could be determined. Now, the team has moved on to the next row of vials. As each vial is opened, the scientists painstakingly put half in the opening and carefully store the other half, keeping another small portion out for study and analysis. The team grows anxious for some additional progress. At first, the addition of the new vials seems ineffective. However, the team carefully readjusts the connectors; the subject of the initial hold up, and after countless adjustments, a constant carrier signal is received. The signal is displayed and fed into a mainframe computer, one linked to larger computer facilities to assist in the deciphering of any possible message.

Lars reviews the progress carefully. True, the team has uncovered only a carrier signal with no modulations, but despite its low intensity, the signal is very real. Lars is nearly beside himself. And it seems that the closer the team gets, the more anxious Lars becomes. He spends the next night restless, even though he is not sure how long it has been since he slept. Lars knows they are getting close. He is certain that the little fellow has a message for them. But how is it transmitted? Will it repeat it over and over? Or will it just give its message and turn off? The messenger has been waiting so long to deliver its message, like a pizza delivery man stuck in the snow. But how do we receive its information? Lars reasons that the answer must lie in the other vials. With this new idea, Lars races back to the project, eager to try a new arrangement.

With nervous excitement, Lars adds the vials slowly, one at a time. With each one, the signal improves, and some modulations are noted. For a moment, the lab waits in silence for the great moment when some word from outer space or long-lost civilization will come to them in some language or code that the linguists and cryptographers can decipher. After a few minutes, the disappointment settles. It is not happening. There is no real message and the scientists have added all the vials.

What to do now? Lars is perplexed, but he remains with the messenger and asks the team to do the same. He will not accept defeat this time. He and his team look over the messenger carefully.

"We must have missed something," he thinks aloud.

As the scientists pour over every detail of the device, Lars looks again at the portals. Lars wonders if the other portals need to be used also, and maybe, just maybe, the messenger is waiting for an input.

Lars' hypothesis seems unlikely to the group of scientists gathered around, but Lars has proven himself time and time again, and they are eager to try anything. The team carefully records the output signal, per Lars' instructions, and plays it back to the little fellow. This has an effect! The team notes a pattern change and again plays back the signal. Another new pattern is revealed. The scientists repeat this process over and over, a little at a time. Each time, they introduce a new variation. Soon, the team clearly understands the game and begins sending more complicated patterns, which are immediately sent back, including the new variations. The scientists rush about, excitedly talking about their next step. Above all this chatter of excitement, the team hears a voice from the back, "Why don't you teach it English? It seems to be a lot smarter than we are."

Lars looks with surprise toward the voice. It is Ellen, the guard again; the same guard who correctly suggested the shell contents was an organic brain.

"Well, there's a good idea," Lars replies. "It's worth a try. Turn on the radio, play it a dictionary, read it books, who knows. This thing is a whole lot smarter than any computer we have."

Happy to be taken seriously, the guard goes on to advise that a children's kindergarten book would be a good place to start. The team agrees, even though the messenger has no visual capabilities. The process proceeds slowly due to this fact, but the little fellow seems to learn at an astonishing rate regardless. The team gathers more complex texts and soon even textbooks for college English courses. The messenger devours each text quickly, and soon, the team recognizes its output signals resemble primitive radio, signals that can be easily converted to understandable English text. There is no need for cryptographers or translators; the messenger is learning English a lot faster than we ever could decode a strange means of communication. Finally, the team can crack open the champagne bottle marked for this occasion. They have achieved a victory, and they know they are infinitely closer to discovering the messenger's purpose. As the room raises their glasses to toast the little fellow, Lars can't help but comment.

"The French will be most unhappy to hear that the first language the little fellow spoke was English. Here's to you."

Laughter spreads across the group, but it is quickly interrupted by a scientist who didn't take a champagne break.

"The messenger wants to learn more! It is asking for more about the human race and if there is any information it could access at a faster transmission speed," the scientist shouts.

"Anything else?" Lars excitedly replies.

"Yes. It asks to have the ambient temperature raised to 40 degrees Celsius."

The team hurriedly puts down their glasses. The work begins again. Lars orders everyone to do as the messenger suggests, and all are eager to comply. Lars, Josh, and everyone involved seem to be mesmerized, and all give this messenger anything it asks for as quickly as they can. Soon, the little fellow can speak English, Spanish, and Latin, and there seems to be no limit to its learning capabilities. It continues to request additional information and it announces that when it has learned more about us, it will be better able to communicate with us. The scientists proceed to learn more about it, discovering its ability to perform many complicated tasks at once. Josh, seeing the phenomenal progress, suggests hooking the little fellow up to a high-speed internet connection. Once connected, the messenger gobbles up every book ever written and accesses science journals, history web pages, religious pages, as well as sites devoted to punk rock. It accesses all the search engines like Google and becomes totally consumed. It appears to have no limits. Not only that, it accomplishes all this at speeds incomprehensible to its observers. The team stands by in awe until the mood is suddenly broken by the messenger stopping its research to make another order, a statement, or maybe a suggestion to the team.

"Set up speakers, a large screen TV, and printers. I want to tell you who I am and why I am here, what I see in your culture and how I can help you."

The team is caught by surprise. True, it is a dream come true that they are communicating, but now, the little thing is giving out orders as if it owns the place. This is unnerving, but Lars is quick to assure the team.

"Maybe we would do best to assume it does own the place."

The team knows Lars is right and proceeds to follow the messenger's instructions. Once the TV and speakers are set up, it asks for a video camera input to one of its connections.

"This way I can see you," it informs them.

Lars is a little taken aback by this statement, but his excitement presses him on as he enters the viewing room for his first interaction.

As the camera pans in on him, Lars begins with his introduction.

"I am the leader of this team, Dr. Lars Anderson," he announces.

"How do you do," responds the messenger.

"Very well," Lars answers, feeling a little awkward speaking to a machine from some world he can only imagine.

The messenger then asks the others for their names and seems interested in each one of them.

"I will now try to tell you all what you want to know as clearly as I can. I was sent here by my makers from the second planet that you call Venus. I was made by the indigenous people of the land before the surface temperature made habitation impossible. I was sent here to tell our children, if you survived, the story of your origin and to warn you of your own demise. My makers sent many probes to the third and fourth planets, Earth and Mars. They determined that the conditions of Earth were possible for their habitation. They also recognized that certain mammalian life forms and humanoids could be potential mates for their species. But the Venusians were never able to actually send a living being; they always sent probes and robots which telecommunicated information back. Their first try at population was in the sea. They captured a fish, close to what you now call dolphins, and mated them with Venusian sperm. The result was a special species with very superior intelligence but little mobility or dexterity."

Lars and the team are awestruck by the messenger's story. Thousands of questions swim in his head, but he knows the messenger still has more to reveal. The messenger continues.

"The next attempts were to capture ape-like creatures, study them and eventually, we were able to impregnate the females with a special frozen sperm which a probe brought from Venus. It was an elaborate plan and was carried out over an extensive period of time. A probe would be launched into an area known to be rich in primates. The primates were lured into a trap, and the females were impregnated and the males neutered and then released. This process continued for over one hundred Earth years. Finally, a new species was born and thrived because of its superior mental and physical abilities. But then, communication to Earth was lost forever, until now."

No one in the room could utter a word. Lars thought he was prepared for anything but definitely not for what he had just heard. He looked to Josh, who returned his glance with the same perplexed amazement. Both knew that the messenger would cause an even greater stir for the theists than they had possibly imagined. But neither could worry about that now. The scientists were sure the messenger had greater purpose than to help humans trace their creation, and they anxiously awaited the rest of its story. Indeed, the messenger continued on for its captivated audience.

"Life on Venus was much like it is here on Earth, clean air, water and freedom to move about. Unfortunately, it was also similar in that it was ruled by corrupt leaders and greedy capitalists. Gradually, the Venusians saw their world change. The greenhouse effect took hold of the planet, and the Venusians were forced to abandon the surface and dig into the heart of their planet to escape the heat and heavy atmosphere caused by the greenhouse effect. Worried about the survival of their race, they established a high-temperature transmitter and receiver system in case their children on Earth wanted to call."

At the completion of this historic conversation, Lars and Josh pledge to each other that they will release only a little information and make secret copies of everything, which can be smuggled out to safe storage, neither of them wanting this information compromised. Undoubtedly, this information is precious but, at the same time, Lars and Josh know that there are many who would not want it to be released to the public. As Lars takes precautions to protect the messenger and its story, he can't help but think of Herdis. He knows how the messenger's story of human creation could shatter her. He wants her to know the truth, but he knows that she, like other people, will need to be introduced slowly to the discovery. Having protected the most controversial information, Lars still meets with his protester committee every day. He looks forward to it, as this is time he gets to spend with Herdis. His love affair with her is definitely on hold, as the monumental events dominate everyone's attention. But he thinks about her and treasures her presence. He feels optimistic about the relationship and feels that Herdis is learning to trust her instincts with him more and more. He only wishes he could share everything with her.

Herdis and the protester group are intently interested in the findings Lars shares, but government guards get more and more restrictive as to what information can be shared and what is considered top secret. Lars feels that the committee is a vital link, and members of the committee naturally feel that they have a right to know such important information. The guards worry about this leak and monitor every word. But Lars feels it is very important to keep the group involved as a part of things, and so far, the military has agreed. So far, all that Lars has been able to release to the public is that the probe is from Venus and it did have a message that we are not alone. Obviously, this is big news all over the world. Lars can't imagine how the world will react when the rest of the messenger's story is revealed. He reasons that the story of how the human was created and went on to prosper and multiply is almost biblical. With a little stretch of the imagination, God could be replaced with the Venusians, and the story of the Garden of Eden is recreated. Perhaps, Lars hopes, this take on the story will help soften the blow. Luckily, Lars has some time to worry about the release of the information. The military is still far more interested in the technology and how it works than in the message itself, and this proves good as it allows for some freedom. Amazingly, everyone is actually settling into some sort of accord. The scientists go about their work; the military tries to enhance its war capabilities; and the theists worry about the truth; but most importantly, the discovery continues.

The little organic computer is far superior to anything we have available. We may have faster computing skills, with our silicon-based technology, but the flexibility, memory capacity, and ability to learn of this little fellow is amazing. The messenger grows much more conversant as time wears on, and everyday, Lars learns more about the demise of the Venusians. The correlation with the situation on Earth alarms everyone. It is difficult but necessary for the team to hear the messenger's story of a civilization destroyed by its own greed and how the powers in control ignored the repeated warnings of their scientists and focused only on their own personal profit and short-term rewards. The only consolation for the scientists drawing the parallels between Earth and Venus is that they are receiving a warning, a privilege the Venusians did not enjoy. Perhaps this could be the difference between life and total destruction.

Lars has long known the outcome of the current state of affairs on Earth. While he hopes the messenger can help change the future, he finds himself more focused on the messenger's stories of the many probes sent to Earth over the years. He realizes that this may mean that there may still be life underground on Venus, and he wonders if contact is still possible, given their receiver system is still powered up. However, Lars faces a great challenge in attempting contact. He needs to get access to a transmitter like the one at Arecibo, but he does not want to release too much information right now. He does have a certain degree of freedom at present; the Government is happy as long as the team is discovering how the technology works and appears busy. But Lars is very anxious to try for the contact and questions whether or not he can communicate his needs to his fellow scientists without tipping off the guards.

Lars decides he must take the chance. He needs a big antenna, and the message needs to be transmitted when the rotation of the Earth and Venus are near opposition for the best communication. Lars and Josh go right to work on programming a message to be sent. They plan for Lars to fly to Puerto Rico alone and send the message with the help of some of his former staff. But since Lars has not left the compound since he first arrived, he is not sure if he will be allowed to leave. He notifies the Government that work cannot continue without some additional resources including several of his books and instruments and that he also needs to recruit some of his former employees. Knowing Lars is instrumental to the continuation of the discovery and that he has the loyalty of the scientific team, the government acquiesces to his request, and Lars is off to Puerto Rico.

Once Lars is back in his old lab, he is much more comfortable. He confides in his former assistant his plans, and together, they recalculate the time code, frequency, and time to send the message. He then quickly returns to the Nevada lab, anxious to not blow his cover story. His staff follows his instructions, uses the code given by the messenger, and plans to broadcast the code toward Venus when the time is right and listen for the answer. After the completion of the broadcast, the staff is supposed to join Lars in Nevada as his new recruits, secretly bringing with them any news from the contact. So far, the plan to make contact has been a success, but all Lars can do now is wait.

CHAPTER VI (EARTH)

Love and Belief

"You are not so afraid of that which you can understand. Ignorance is the real enemy," remarks Lars conclusively at the end of yet another meeting with the protest group.

Lars feels he is making progress. The protesters seem to be responding to the project with an open mind, and Lars knows that communication is the key to keeping the situation under control. But while the group seems satisfied with the limited information Lars provides, the media has been frantic to learn about the message. As a matter of fact, the protest camp has been inundated with media and now resembles a temporary city. Luckily, Lars' attempt to limit the media and his overseers' knowledge of his progress in understanding the message has been working so far. The overseers of the project remain more interested in how the organic computer works, and Lars placates them by providing information on its construction and possible methods of duplication. The media, however, is relentless. Fortunately, their access is limited by the government, and Lars retains control over the dissemination of information. He is enjoying a reprieve at the moment, with the media being held at bay and by the fact that the real science is now occurring at Lars' old lab in Arecibo. His old team makes a furious effort to locate and communicate with the underground people of Venus, now known to be our very forefathers, parents, and origins. Lars has yet to hear from his team, and while the anticipation consumes him, he finds more time to concentrate on things he has been forced to ignore.

As the protest group prepares to leave the meeting, Lars looks for Herdis in the crowd. Because of her, he has been taking extra care to keep the group as informed as the censors will allow. True, he is still safeguarding much of the message, but during this meeting, he revealed the story of the plight of the people of Venus. Of course, he has not yet explained that we are their offspring or that the group at Arecibo is trying to contact them. He found that telling the group this information was challenging enough, knowing that this information may have been difficult for some of the group members. He is a little concerned about

Herdis and anxious to see how she is feeling. He notices her across the room and hoping to take her mind off the meeting, he decides to invite her for another run. Fully expecting another refusal, he approaches her. To his surprise, she smiles at him and accepts his offer. As the time is set and she walks away, Lars can barely contain himself.

The run is very pleasant, and it is obvious that Lars and Herdis truly enjoy one another's company. They joke back and forth about their differences, but they also notice that they seem to still fit together.

"I actually used to have an organized list of questions based on my studies in psychology that I would ask all women. I even had a rating system based on age, interests, sibling relations, and so on," Lars confides to Herdis at the end of their running date.

Herdis can't help but laugh. "A true scientist," she remarks smiling.

"But," Lars rebuts, "You have to admit I've come a long way since that rating system. I've known you were the one since you smiled and ran past me in that Half Marathon run in Las Vegas. And," Lars remarks smiling, "I didn't even need an organized system of lists and formulas to tell me that."

"Why, I guess you have made progress," Herdis replies, happy to hear that Lars shares her feelings. But one question continues to plague her; how can he be the one when they have such differing views? She decides to test his openness.

"I don't suppose for our next date you would like to attend church with me?" she asks nervously.

"Well, I haven't been for years, and, while it isn't at the top of my list, I suppose it could be interesting. Sure, I'll go with you. I'll pick you up tomorrow."

Herdis departs, simply consumed with happiness. "Maybe it can work after all," she thinks optimistically.

Lars watches Herdis head for the protesters' city. He knows that it is important for him to understand her beliefs, and it helps him to know that while she is a Christian believer of the basic sort, she possesses a true love of peace and her fellow man. Lars finds this quality to be a rarity among followers of Jesus Christ, although his message was to love thy enemy, turn the other cheek, and give both coats away. None of the major organizations espousing Christianity seem to follow these basic teachings of the master. Herdis, on the other hand, is a true Christian, not a Bible-toting, preacher-type who goes to church on Sunday and then robs, cheats, molests, and steals the rest of the week. Nor is she the type to believe that if you make a big enough tithing to the church, you will buy yourself a seat at the right hand of the almighty. Quite to the contrary, Lars notes, Herdis follows a simple, genuine philosophy of giving to help others and working for peace and love of all mankind, not just one particular race or ethnicity. Lars thinks Herdis might be the wisest Christian he has ever met, and he admires her honesty and dedication.

The next day, as Lars is putting on his Sunday best, he realizes that he is a little nervous about his church date. He hasn't worn much other than a lab coat for some time, and he is not sure how he will react to the services. As he goes to pick up Herdis, he can hardly believe the power she has over him; it amazes him that a beautiful woman can be so influential. But as she runs toward him, his previous thoughts are forgotten, and he finds himself happy to oblige her.

At the service, Lars notices that there is only a handful of devotees, all very genuine and loving folks, but all very different and there for different reasons. Lars feels very much out of place, even though he is happy to find no icons, crosses dripping with blood, or self-appointed clergy directing the worship. As he takes his seat next to Herdis, the service begins as a peaceful older lady moves to the front of the room. She softly asks everyone to hold hands and focus their energies toward goodness and righting the wrongs of the world. Lars certainly has no objection, and, as a matter of fact, he actually feels the energy flowing through the circle. He is not too surprised; he has studied the scientific reports about the power of prayer and hands on healing. The only problem he sees is that the power of prayer has nothing to do with any religious cults or rituals; even an Atheist could it. There is no need for God, just a spirit of true love and a real desire to do good, in order for the object of the prayer to be accomplished.

At the end of the service, Herdis and Lars exit hand in hand. She is overjoyed by his participation and hopes she can open his mind as he has opened hers. In the same way his skillful explanations and communication have changed her mind about the little messenger she once thought was the devil, perhaps she can help him discover the power of faith. Lars just reduces every feeling to a logical reason, tries to understand it, and then devises tests for his hypotheses. Herdis sees the value in his methods but can't help but feel he is missing out on so much more that cannot be boiled down to scientific facts.

"Why do we want to believe in him or her or it?" Lars suddenly asks Herdis, obviously analyzing the experience he has just had at church.

"What do you mean by that?" Herdis asks, knowing there is much more behind Lars' question.

"There has never been any documented reason to believe in God," Lars continues. "When I was a youngster growing up as a Catholic, I went to cataclysm class in order to receive my First Holy Communion. I remember that the first question in our book was, "Who made the world?" I myself thought that was a very good question. The answer the book gave was, 'God made the world'. And then the next question was, 'How do we know God made the world?' I thought that question was even better. The answer in the book was, 'The Bible told us so'. It seemed to me, even as a child, that the next logical question was, 'How do we know the bible is true?' So I asked the priest this very question. The next day, the priest showed up at my mother's house to ask that I not attend the catechism class any more as I was too disruptive."

"And so that was the end of religion for you?" Herdis asks.

"More like the beginning, I'd say. After that experience, I went to work analyzing religious beliefs and outlining the facts."

"Of course you did," Herdis jokes. "I suppose there is a dissertation somewhere with all your arguments laid out in proper scientific fashion."

"As a matter of fact," Lars begrudgingly admits, "It's more like an essay."

"May I read it?" Herdis asks, now quite serious and honestly interested in knowing more about Lars' beliefs.

"Yes, I suppose you should," Lars answers.

Lars is nervous the entire drive back to his house. He has never let anyone read his essay, but he feels that if he and Herdis are to last, that he must be as open and honest with his beliefs as she has been with hers. He agrees to go to his quarters and see if he can find a copy or print her a copy from his personal computer. Lars returns shortly and hands her the essay, she looks at it briefly and then back at him with a comforting smile. Lars breathes a sigh of relief, he knows he can trust her and he realizes that this is a necessary step in their relationship. He sits close to her as she begins to read.

Lars Anderson's Essay

THIS I, LARS ANDERSON, BELIEVE:

To address the big question, "Is there a GOD?", we need to define what we are asking. By God, do we mean a Supreme Being, creator of Heaven and Earth, or are we referring to a lesser, subservient God who just meddles around in a few chosen human lives? (This was the God of the Old Testament). Let us consider each of these cases separately.

All societies have created some type of higher deity. Some are omnipotent, flawless, and/or the Creator, and some have considerable failings and limitations. So we need to look for some truth to be able to establish the existence of this supernatural being, besides our personal desire for a figure head to worship. There are several approaches to this question. One is to cite the facts as we would all agree to them. Second, we can survey the claims of the various proponents of religions, cults, and early civilizations. We should give more weight to the earlier aboriginal societies since they may be the closest to any real spiritual connection to the idea of the God figurehead. We should look for a commonality among all these entities. We need only to establish a miracle or two or some other testable and reproducible happenings to confirm the existence of the deity. So far, this has not been done.

To sell themselves, most religions offer eternal life, transcendence to the after life of some sort. The proponents tell us that we must have FAITH. BUT WHY?? If the religion is true, what's with faith? Let us see the sign. The evidence, the golden tablets, a reproducible miracle or two, even a universality of feeling would be impressive, and actually, the latter may well exist but is masked by all the ritual and false myths, icons, and witchcraft.

What do we really know? We only have input from our five senses: sight, hearing, smell, touch, and taste. These input to a computer of significant design capabilities, the brain, which then runs the machine we call a human being and provides him or her with all knowledge, that is, UNLESS we want to stretch to another means of input such as PSI or instinct (whatever that means) or divine communication. (*continued next page*)

Serious arguments have been made along these lines, and some interesting experiments have shown anomalies such as remote viewing, precognition, weight transients at the moment of death, and the work at the PEAR Lab in Princeton. All these studies hint at some force beyond our understanding. But is that enough to conclude it is God?

When discussing this subject with devotees, believers, and addicts, mainly Christian because these are far more numerous among my associations, you can see that they really believe what they are saying, even though it does not make much sense. They hear "a music" or a message, have an awakening, feel a born-again zeal; it must be beautiful. I feel like a rat in Hamlin that is deaf and cannot hear the music of the Pied Piper who is piping all the rats into the sea.

I know these well-meaning people really believe that they hear the music. But I am reminded of an old saying, "Never trust someone who carries only ONE book." The Bible is just one book. I must admit that the sincerity of these folks is impressive and must be considered. Why are they so adamant? Did they get the word from on high? Are there others who are inspired the same way? Do they all sing the same song? Starting with the last, I am inclined to answer, "NO, definitely not." There are almost as many religions as there are societal groups in the world. Some have been unified by war and economics, but most disagree on even the most fundamental issues. BUT they all hear the music. How do we explain that?

Each human is born with an innate desire to be a part of the group. This served us well during the early caveman days and now manifests itself as religion. Religion serves many functions. It unites people into a common line of thinking. It serves as a social center, and it reports to answer the big questions such as: Where did we come from? Why are we here? And where are we going? Some religions resort to magic, miracles, witchcraft, and the like. All practice an agenda of brainwashing. It is essential to keep the flock together and increasing in numbers, strength, money, and power.

Of course, all these negatives do not answer the question. Do you hear the music? Do I hear the music? Do we hear the music? You MUST extricate yourself from the conventional religious trappings and mythologies taught to you by your parents, priests, and elders who do not know any more about this subject than you do. The truth shall ONLY be found within yourself. Within each of us is a feeling of being a part of the universe. We belong here; we are doing what we are supposed to be doing. This commune of feeling is the real thing. If there is a spiritual world out there, it can only be accessed through these feelings and NOT through huge religious apparatus designed to numb your sensitivities, pick your pocket, and deafen your ability to hear the music.

I do not know if there is a spiritual world beyond our understanding or not, but I do know that all religions are a fabrication of man.

As Herdis finishes reading the letter, she hands it back to Lars. He looks at her expectantly, waiting for her response.

She looks back at him and begins, "Thank you for sharing your ideas with me. The point I would have to argue the strongest is that I believe it is wrong to challenge the Bible, which is the word of God."

"How do we know the Bible is the word of God?" Lars replies, the same question plaguing him since childhood. "And," he continues, "what do we really know about Jesus Christ? Whether he was a myth or a real historical person matters little. The fact is that it was 70 AD, almost 40 years minimum after his death, before his words were reduced to writing. During this period, stories were told from father to son, legends were created, and the truth faded into the background in a mist of ideas, wonderment, and hopes. In fact, the writing of the gospels was almost a cottage industry in the early days. Only later did they select the ones that suited their needs. So, you see, the Bible shouldn't be taken quite so literally or seen as an unbiased work."

Lars stops for a moment, realizing he may have gone a bit too far. He notices the look of concern on Herdis' face, and he softens his tone before continuing on. It pains him to have to see her upset, but he must be honest with her.

"How can we now," Lars explains, "two thousand years later, rediscover the teachings of this quiet carpenter whose ideas changed the world? The only record is the Holy Bible, a book written, rewritten, translated, and agonized over by many individuals and organizations, all with different agendas and goals. A review of the Bibles currently available will show a vast discrepancy in text and message. There have been many very earnest efforts to recreate the text as faithfully as possible, and scholars have toiled at this for two thousand years. But how can we sift through, weed out, and to try to separate the wheat from the chaff, in order to decide the true message of the Bible?"

Herdis is quick with her rebuttal. "I understand that the Bible cannot be taken literally in all senses. But how do you explain its existence in the first place or the great effort by so many people to preserve its teachings? The Bible has survived for centuries because it is the word of God. People know this in their hearts, despite a few discrepancies and some minor modifications."

"But these discrepancies are important," Lars argues. "The Old Testament, which is a history of the Jewish people, is a testament, a covenant, and agreement with the God of the Jews and the Jewish people, which as the Old Testament accounts, has been broken repeatedly by both parties. The Old Testament is a history, and a very bloody history at that, of the Jewish people. It is filled with the vilest sorts of misbehavior, most of which is condoned by their God. It is clear that the God of the Old Testament is ONLY the God of the circumcised, the Jewish people, and did not serve any others. When did this God get promoted to cover the world?"

Herdis looks at Lars in wonder. "But," she remarks, "you aren't considering the teachings of Jesus Christ."

Lars is not sure that he and Herdis will ever agree on this subject. But he is starting to enjoy the friendly debate and pushes on.

"I am getting to that. Let's say," Lars proceeds, "that you consider the only the three synoptic Gospels of the Bible. Starting with the earliest text first, you find 'The Gospel According to Mark' written a little before AD 70, a simple story of a miracle worker and his teachings of humility, loving your oppressor, and turning the other cheek. He was born of normal poor parents. For his efforts, he was crucified and then, according to legend, he was resurrected. Matthew follows and contains much of the same information of Mark, with the addition of accounts of a virgin birth and the lineage of Jesus to the house of David. This, as you know, was a requirement of the Old Testament prophecy of the coming of the Messiah. Matthew wished to portray Jesus as this Messiah since this Gospel was aimed at Jews he wished to convert Christians. Later, around AD 80, comes Luke who was thought to be a Gentile, and again, the focus was shifted to appeal to the conversion of the Gentiles. Luke ignores the virgin birth, as well as The Old Testament prophecies. The Romans are treated more kindly, and the Jews are shown to be the villains. The last Gospel is John, which is written much later, around 100 to 150 AD, and is probably far less reliable as a source of the original message. In John, Jesus is elevated to a Godly persona, and the humble carpenter is forgotten. John includes the virgin birth and also elevates Mary to a figure of worship. This suits a growing Christian Church with all its trappings and church domination of local life. In John, you can also clearly see the influence of Paul of Tarsus and the motive of church building."

Herdis is unsure where Lars is going with his explanation. "But don't you see that, since the same events unfold in each, there must be some truth behind them, despite a few inconsistencies here and there?" Lars is hardly finished, but he appreciates Herdis' interest and her sound objections. His respect for her grows, as most refuse to even engage in debate with him over his religious views. He truly admires her dedication and her belief, even though he cannot quite understand it. He is anxious to share more of his thoughts, not so much to convince her, but to explain where he is coming from.

"I don't know about truth. But I do know that in order to determine what Jesus actually said, we do need to look at Mark, Matthew, and Luke. Also the gospel of Thomas, which contradicts Luke, should be considered. Jesus taught that the New Testament or covenant was at hand and that an era of new thinking was needed if you wished to sit with his father in heaven for eternity. Jesus taught that the Old Testament idea of 'an eye for an eye' was wrong and that we need to go forward to turn the other cheek, give both your shirt and your coat, and the like. This was the essence of the new teachings of John the Baptist and then, more eloquently, of Jesus. Jesus proposed a New Testament, a new covenant-love thy enemy. If you want to read Jesus' true message, you should refer to Mathew 5:40-42, 6:1, 19:21 and Luke 6:27-30 and 9:25. The rest of the New Testament was written by second-generation church founders from the ideas of Paul, who never knew Jesus, the master."

"I agree that those passages are the most significant teachings of the Lord. It sounds as if you believe some of the Bible is truly factual," Herdis remarks, glad to finally agree on something.

"Correlating, but not necessarily factual," Lars clarifies.

"It sounds as if your problem is not so much with Jesus or the truth of his existence but with the other church leaders," Herdis replies.

"You could say that. It was Paul that was ultimately responsible for the success of the Catholic Church and all of the other splinter groups. He gave it structure and coated it with blood and suffering. This all seems very human to an outside observer. The other major religions of the earth, under careful examination, do not fare any better. They are all derived from ancient legends and are all without any credible validation. Now, it is true that a large portion of the world's population believes in one or more of these mythologies. Why? Because there is a basic need within each of us to have connect with the ONE, the maker, the mother, the eternal spirit, the creator, God. We need to know or want to know where we fit into the scheme of things. Where did we come from? Where are we going? Why are we here? What type of life should we live? All the popular religions try, in one way or another, to answer these questions and give their adherents an afterlife, a hope, and more importantly, a sense of belonging to a group. In religion, the facts do not really matter; it usually is what one generation teaches the next. This is why religions are so afraid of the truth, fear new ideas, and restrict the activities of their cult members by creating their own schools to inculcate the young and prohibit out of faith marriages."

"But it is not religion that answers the questions about where we are from and who we are. I already know and feel it. It is hard for me to accept your confusion. For me, it is something that I just know, deep down, in my soul. Perhaps your bad experiences with religion have led you to deny yourself the truth of Jesus Christ; that you have blocked him out because of your bad experiences with organized religion," Herdis remarks with a softness in her voice.

"I will agree," Lars answers, "that if Jesus had a chance to do any editing to the Bible, it would read a whole lot different. And if he were in charge of the flock, its behavior would be very different. If Jesus were here now and in charge of 'his church,' what would the church do? How would they act toward others? How would they help the poor? Would they build those huge churches or give the funds to those in need? The truth is that the whole thing is human and not divine. All religion is human endeavor."

Herdis looks at Lars patience and compassion. She is done arguing. She is impressed with his knowledge and was happy to listen to his tirade. Maybe now that she knows his struggle with faith and where it originates, she can help him find his way back to the Lord.

Lars, on the other hand, looks back at Herdis from an entirely different perspective. Before him, he sees a misguided young girl that needs saving herself. Only she needs to be saved from irrational cult worship that is interfering with his courtship efforts. Lars finds it interesting that Herdis had not interrupted nor protested too much when Lars pointed out the obvious failings of the Bible and the horrible history of murder, mass killings, and exterminations carried out in the name of the church. But perhaps she is so riveted in faith that her communion with the almighty allows her to forgive the inconsistencies Lars described. Yes, Lars reasons, though the church may be untrue, the Bible a mere work of man, and Jesus Christ a fiction, her faith is true and strong within her. She knows she has something special, and her religion allows her to access the spirit she knows is there. Lars cannot and will not argue with that. In fact, he knows that Herdis is truly in touch with some divine, serene entity. He can see it in her eyes and in her gentle manner. He would not want to change that pure feeling. She has a gift, and he will definitely have to take another look at the whole picture and reassess it.

As the two continue to talk and the night wears on, both realize that they are falling in love despite of their differences. They have a mutual respect for each other's point of view, and while they disagree on many points, the other is happy to listen to the opposing side. In fact, they both find that the controversy stimulates and excites them, a challenge that they have both found lacking in previous relationships.

As Lars heads to the lab the next morning, he is bursting with joy. His mind is moving a mile a minute, and he is focused on addressing this new, most important thing in his life, wooing Herdis. But he has never really attacked such a problem and his skills are certainly limited in this field. He has done some of the right things and a lot of wrong things through the years, being so rational is not always advantageous in the love department. After much contemplation, he decides on a frontal assault. But he realizes he needs help. He calls on the advice of his friend and confidant, Josh, who has had a lot more experience in these matters.

"Buy her flowers," Josh suggests, "and take her to a starlit, secluded spot and run out of gas."

Lars rolls his eyes, but he realizes that Josh may be right. "But," he asks his friend, "how can such a rational fellow do all this?"

Josh just laughs at poor Lars. He is happy to see Lars excited about something other than the messenger. He definitely needs a break from the headache at the lab. Seeing Lars so thrilled certainly makes Josh miss his family. But at least there will be something else to talk about at work. Josh heads back to his project, watching Lars head out the door to prepare for his date.

Lars gets to work, packing up his SUV with some goose-down sleeping bags, a bottle of champagne, a beautiful gold necklace, a supply of smoked salmon, cream cheese, and sourdough bread while he sends out a courier for the best flowers in town. As he packs up a small table and chairs into the back, he starts feeling like he is doing some sort of strange mating ritual, like grebes that skitter across the water to impress their potential mate, or like a frog trying to croak the loudest or sing the most beautiful songs.

"This must be some ancient ritual," he thinks to himself. "Here I am right in there with the frogs and grebes and all God's (whoops, better watch my language) creatures."

While Lars does not really understand this ritual mating game and really doesn't have time for it, he does find it a little fun. After all, he is acutely aware that he is hooked, in love, and needs to do whatever it takes to win her over. With the preparations complete, Lars proceeds to drive over to pick Herdis up at the designated time of 6 PM sharp. As she climbs in, Lars surprises her with his plans.

"There is a comet that will appear, so I brought a small telescope to view it," Lars informs her.

"Sounds perfect," she replies, excited for the evening ahead.

Lars has already reconnoitered the area and found the perfect spot in the desert where they would not be disturbed. With his position and with all the security around, Lars certainly does not want to be caught in some compromising circumstance. He pulls up to his chosen location, unloads the table and chairs, sets the table, and poured the champagne. The view of the stars and the quiet of the desert seem perfect, and Lars smiled at Herdis.

She looks back at him, reflecting his feelings. "I'm not really a drinker," she says noticing the champagne, "but I'll keep you company."

"Well, I guess I'll have to drink the whole bottle," Lars replies with a gentle laugh.

As the evening progresses, Lars can't stop thinking about how perfect everything is, out under the stars with the love of his life. The comet appears as predicted; he was good at that. Then, he rolls out the sleeping bags and hopes that his plan is not too obvious. He is afraid he will spook her like a deer in the woods. But she responds as if she wants the same, just cuddling up to him as if this is the way it should be. He kisses her many times, and they blend together. Soon, they are nude in the comfy down sleeping bags, and her body is totally responsive and feels wonderful. He feels all of her, and it is wonderful and greater that anything he has ever experienced. They lay together all night, enjoying a bonding beyond description. He does not even attempt to have sex; there will be time for that later. He simply wants to savor this very special moment. And as he looks up at the stars with her body lying close to his, he thinks in his infinite happiness, "Wow. I don't even need an instruction book for this."

CHAPTER VII (EARTH)

Chocolate

With the meal carts rolled away and the lights dimmed, most of the passengers on the red-eye flight to Puerto Rico are sleeping soundly. Lars Anderson, on the other hand, remains upright and alert, busily pouring through the files he brought aboard. He can hardly find room to organize his documents, much less his thoughts. Twelve hours ago, he was performing his typical daily tasks at the lab, monitoring the messenger and managing his team. Things had been progressing as usual until the messenger made a very unexpected special announcement.

"I have decided to give myself a name. From now on, I wish to be addressed as Chocolate," the probe had stated to its eager audience.

Lars smiled remembering this.

"Why Chocolate?" they had asked.

"After talking to all of you that have been taking care of me and reviewing the internet, I have determined that the one thing everyone likes is this stuff you call chocolate."

Certainly, no one could disagree and all found the little messenger's name to be perfectly suited. But it was not the new name that sent Lars rushing back to Puerto Rico on the next available flight. Shortly after Chocolate announced his appellation, he declared that he wanted to tell his story again, but with further instructions.

"As I explained before," Chocolate began, "I was launched long ago by the fathers of the human race to explain to the humans, when they reached technical maturity, who their parents were, where they came from, and where they may be going. I was sent along with six other probes, which you still may find from time to time. Our mission is to tell our story. If you have reached technical maturity in time, you may even be able to contact your parents on Venus and possibly rescue them from their underground habitat. I would estimate the surface temperature now to be around 300 degrees Celsius (572 F), so you would need launch capability to transport digging equipment to Venus capable of working at that temperature. There were receivers installed on the surface at various locations to receive any possible message from their children in case they were capable of calling home. But from the unclassified literature, I am not sure you are capable of this task at this time. I suggest you send a message with the following information. Please record exactly as I give it."

At the time, Lars nearly jumped off his stool with excitement. He was coming so much closer to his dream; he could almost feel it happening. He found it difficult to conceal the work he had already secretly done toward making contact, but still managed to obtain the details of the frequency and antenna requirements to send such a momentous message. He asked Chocolate where they should send the message from and Chocolate informed the team that he had surveyed all the major transmitters and decided the one at Arecibo would be best suited. Lars could hardly believe his luck. Deciding that this mission to communicate with Venus was too important for him not to be directly involved, Lars had jumped on the next plane to Puerto Rico. He wanted to be right there if contact was made.

With Lars on his way to Arecibo, Josh Van Dever carefully maintains control of the messenger back in Nevada, the primary responsibilities at the lab having fallen to him in Lars' absence. For now, he and his team must devote all resources to documenting Chocolate's messages. Chocolate now converses quite freely with everyone on almost any subject and seems better informed in nearly every field than even the greatest specialists. Josh is careful to monitor every word. He is determined not to miss one valuable insight from this visitor, even though Chocolate has taken to making unsolicited insults as of late. As Josh files the last of his reports and heads toward the research lab, he hears Chocolate at it again.

"You are still primitive creatures with little regard for the environment in which you live. You have no respect for life," Chocolate openly remarks to the room.

Josh hurriedly enters the lab, and he feels sorry that Lars is missing this. Surely, Lars would love to hear Chocolate's true observations. But something bothers Josh about this type of communication from Chocolate. Josh knows that Chocolate is speaking true wisdom, but he is also aware that humanity does not take criticism well. He worries that, when Chocolate is heard by the public, they will react poorly to his straightforward observations. Uncertain if Chocolate will understand Josh's attempt to mitigate his remarks, Josh approaches Chocolate.

"I realize you possess great knowledge," Josh begins. "But humans are not used to accepting such a harsh critique."

Chocolate, unaware of any wrongdoing, replies, "I make no apologies for my observations. It is you that should re-examine why you deserve the criticism I give. For example, you have a sport you call hunting where you kill animals just to see them die. It is a reenactment of ancient predatory skills used for survival in the caveman days."

Josh quickly realizes that Chocolate will not understand the reason for his request. He sighs in frustration, only to be interrupted by Chocolate once again. Apparently, this conversation is not over.

"You kill each other without regard in wars, uprisings, exterminations, inquisitions, prison camps, killing fields, and slaughter innocents, and yet there is an enormous cultural struggle about an unborn fetus. Why kill millions and worry about a fetus? Why do you disrupt meaningful medical research by freeing primates, rats, dogs, etcetera, and then raise, fatten, and slaughter billions of animals for food? Either life is important or it is not. You are certainly a hypocritical species."

Josh couldn't agree more. But what can he say? Should he really ask Chocolate to soften the truth? Before he can muster up a response, Chocolate continues on.

"It is obvious to an external observer such as myself that the human race is at a crossroads. Your technological development has far surpassed your social development. The system of rational thinking, which has served the physical sciences so well, has provided all the progress you now enjoy. The biological and medical sciences have thus far not adapted the rigorous rational norms that worked so well for the physical sciences. This is mainly because the medical field evolved from witch doctors, shamans, and medicine men, some of whom were very skilled but all of whom lacked the discipline of modern science. To this day, most medical research is directed by the non-scientists like doctors-people trained in treating injured and sick patients and not trained in the scientific method. This has restricted medical advances and limited both the quality and length of human life. There exists a triumvir of the doctors, the Pharmaceutical Companies, and the Health Insurance Companies to control the access to healthcare at enormous profits to themselves."

Chocolate awaits a response from the scientists crowded around, but everyone is speechless. Many of the scientists are not surprised by Chocolate's observations, and many have observed the same. However, no one seems to have an explanation for this corrupt behavior by humans. After several moments of silence, Josh gives instructions to the current crew to closely record any further dialogue and sends the others home for a few hours of rest. He retires to his office, his mind full of questions and finding no answers to Chocolate's poignant questions. As he reviews the record of the day's findings, he realizes he hasn't spoken to Lars since he landed. He hurriedly picks up the phone and dials Lars at the lab in Arecibo.

"How's it going down there? Any news?" Josh asks excitedly.

"Still setting up. What is happening on your end?" Lars replies.

"He's growing extremely talkative, sharing a lot of insights with us. But I'm worried about how the public will take his messages when it comes to that."

"Brutal honesty can be rough. How is the protest group responding?" Lars inquires, anxious to hear any news of Herdis.

"You think we should involve them in the dialogue?" Josh is hesitant.

"Wait until I return. I will wrap things up here in a few days."

Lars sets down the receiver and finds himself more anxious than ever to return to the lab. He never imagined he would miss Herdis this much, especially with such an exciting project to occupy his time. He gathers his current research team and provides them with the new, more detailed information from Chocolate. With this information, the correct time and direction of the transmission can be calculated. The crew sets right to work, and Lars informs every one of Chocolate's latest revelations which he receives from Josh nearly every hour by fax. The team works non-stop, and within a day, the transmission is ready for sending, and a message is sent. They wait in anticipation, but no answer is received. They try again and again, each time losing a little hope.

"Well, I guess there's nothing new about that. We have had that result for many years. But this is the first time we have tried to contact at a known code and frequency," Lars remarks, not hiding his disappointment.

But just as Lars finishes his thoughts, their sent message relays back to them, loud and clear. Measurements confirm that it is a signal generated from Venus. No one is sure whether the signal is from a real entity or from a robot programmed to respond. The team tries a slight variance on the original message and receives a similarly varied response in return. Several more messages are sent, and with each message, the answer is identical to the transmitted message. This echo response surprises Lars, but the fact remains that the message definitely comes from a transmitter on the surface of Venus. Thrilled by the success, Lars hurriedly contacts Josh, hoping Chocolate can provide more information. Chocolate tells the team that the antennas were programmed to respond to the input message.

"In fact," Chocolate discloses, "the antennas may be on automatic, and there may be no one left alive."

This is sad news, but Chocolate hasn't erased all hope yet. He volunteers the coordinates of the antenna at Northern Latitude 15 degrees and Longitude of 274 degrees and says that there could be a possibility of contact with the community, if they were still alive, if they were to dig below the antenna. In addition, he offers to provide detailed drawings of the underground facilities and offers to assist in the planning of a rescue mission.

With the latest maps of the Venusian surface, the scientists easily identify the exact location Chocolate references. Josh, Lars, and the Puerto Rico scientists carefully safeguard this information, in case the overseers become unreasonable. This contact is monumental, and all fear what the government may do if it discovers how close Arecibo has gotten. With the information safely stored in various locations, Lars packs his bags and sets out for Nevada, anxious to see the progress back at the lab and even more anxious to see Herdis again. First contact has been accomplished, and Lars couldn't be happier as he boards his flight.

To Lars' dismay, however, it is Josh that greets him at the airport. A part of him hoped Herdis would be waiting for him, but he knows he will see her soon. Josh takes Lars back to the lab where Lars enjoys a visit with Chocolate. Chocolate has become increasingly talkative and quite wise. Lars asks for Chocolate's latest revelation about human society, and Chocolate begins one of his famous insights.

"The worst problem I see is in the social sciences where ancient tradition, ethnic customs, ruthless leaders, ignorance, and intolerance rule. Research in these fields is nonexistent. No progress can be made under these conditions. Dominance still prevails everywhere. There are even places on your planet where discrimination, subjugation of women, concentration of the assets in the hands of a few, slavery, and other ancient unsocial behavior is encouraged and enforced. WHY?"

Chocolate expects no answer, and Lars certainly doesn't have one. As he documents the observation Chocolate has just made, he can't help but laugh to himself. Chocolate certainly never lets anyone off the hook. He can finally see what Josh meant by the public not being ready for such harsh criticism of their society. But Chocolate's revelations have to be heard, especially ones like Lars had just witnessed about systems of dominance. The more we understand these systems, the better our chance of survival. But how to unfold these truths to the public, and is the world ready? He begins to wonder if they are all in the presence of some kind of Tree of Knowledge.

"Do we eat the fruit? Is it good to know these things?" Lars asks himself. "Thanks to Chocolate, we can all look into the future with accuracy. But are we really ready?"

Lars is not sure if he will ever know. Perhaps these things take thousands of years to get used to. Unfortunately, with the government breathing down his neck, Lars doesn't feel he has too much time before he has to let Chocolate speak to the public. He has always dreamed of being one of the pioneers to make the first encounter, and now, it is unfolding right before his eyes. Yet he hesitates, not sure what may be learned. The world is uncomfortable with new ways of breaking tradition, but that is the very nature of what science does, so Lars ultimately concludes that there is nothing else to do but move forward. He decides that the first step is to allow his protest group some interaction with Chocolate and schedules an immediate meeting.

Herdis arrives at the meeting, and she is more beautiful than Lars remembers. True, it has only been a few days since he's seen her, but the sight of her fills him with unimaginable joy. The smile on her face indicates that she is filled with the same passion. Lars struggles a little at the meeting, unable to take his eyes off her. The others notice, and Lars is forced to compose himself.

"The probe has learned our language, actually 57 languages so far, and has told us its origin and that there may still be survivors living on Venus. Further, I will let you talk with him. He has now given himself a name and wishes to be addressed as Chocolate. You are free to ask him anything you may like."

The room remains silent. All three members of the protest group are in great shock and also quite scared by this opportunity to talk to this thing from outer space. But, in their fear, there is also great excitement. The group is led by Lars into the lab where Chocolate is waiting for them. Lars feels the tension, and wonders who will begin. Slowly, the creationist takes a step forward and in a tentative voice, uncomfortably addresses Chocolate.

"If you don't mind, I would like to ask you about creationism and the origin of Cro-Magnon man."

Without missing a beat, Chocolate immediately replies.

"The theory of creationism is espoused to try to change the 'facts' when they do not agree with a certain mythical story or belief. However, you have touched on an anomaly of human evolution. What happened to what you call Neanderthal man? Actually, Neanderthal was our creation, but unfortunately, he contained a genetic defect, which we eliminated in a later and our last model, you. So, it was the defect that eliminated Neanderthal. The people of Venus are the creators of the human race as it now exists. However, this in no way negates your beliefs in the existence of transcendent forces that are the basis of many beliefs, yours included."

The creationist is frozen in his tracks by this frighteningly frank and accurate and probably true assessment of his question. But Chocolate is not finished.

"You will soon find that you yourselves have to take up the art of creation, via cloning. You know the two-gender system evolved in order to provide a means of genetic variation and adaptation of the species to a changing environment. It provided the tools for evolution. That was until mankind developed sufficient skills to be able to alter their own genetic structure. At this point, cloning is desirable, and in the future, it will be essential and mandatory. The earth's resources are limited, and careful population design and control will be required within the next fifty Earth years."

Lars is sure that no one was ready to hear that response. But the alternative is to have Chocolate's great insights kept from the very people that need to hear them. Cautiously, he signals to the next protester that it is time for his question. He approaches nervously.

"What can we do to save our environment?" he asks quietly, fearful of the answer.

"Limit the right to procreate, stop burning fossil fuels, and protect your air and water. No more burning of anything. Manage your forests to eliminate fire. Use only clean energy like nuclear, tidal, solar, wind, and hydro. Shut down every gas, coal, and oil-fired power plant and replace them with nuclear plants today. Dam up every stream. Put out every fire. To try to save endangered species flies in the face of nature, which eliminates billions of species every day. You now have the power to save DNA material of any species you may wish to recreate, and you can also alter any species, so why waste pure clean water to save fish? The water is needed to generate clean electricity, irrigate the fields, and to supply the thirsty cities."

Herdis cringes at the thought of it being her turn. Lars looks at her and notices that she is not ready. She wants to ask, "Is there a God?" but she knows she is not ready for the answer.

"Could I possibly ask my question later?" she whispers, nervously awaiting Lars' response.

Lars nods with a smile. She really could have asked for anything, and he would have agreed.

"I really do want to ask. I'm just not quite ready now. Are you sure I can return later?" Herdis inquires, wanting to confirm that she is not losing her chance to question the oracle.

"I promise, Herdis," Lars replies, touching her shoulder, and they smile at each other as the group is led back to the gates outside.

As they return to the protester camp, each member of the group realizes the grave responsibility they have been given. A great change has come over the entire group, including Lars. A spirit of cooperation and joint effort to seek the truth has grown out of this unlikely alliance. Lars can't help but think that if this little diverse group who was initially so opposed to all of this could now work together, maybe there was hope for the world.

"I'm happy that I could finally share this with you," Lars confides in Herdis.

But before Herdis can reply, Josh comes running toward Lars.

"Sorry to interrupt, but we need you inside. NASA has found out about the contact, and they are here to see you."

Lars quickly says a quick goodbye to Herdis and hurries to the lab. There, he finds NASA scientists crawling all over. Unlike the military, NASA is a welcome participant in the project, especially now that the coordinates for a shuttle mission have been determined. The NASA scientists find Chocolate easy to communicate with, and the staff grows to enjoy the contacts and the wisdom they receive with each one. The same, of course, is true for the Army's scientific team, but Lars still feels anger toward the people that originally wanted to dismantle the probe and figure out what made it tick. Luckily for the project, Chocolate's communication skills prompt all who encounter him to find that they can learn all they want just by asking, and their fears are allayed, and as a result, security is relaxed. Chocolate seems to have a calming effect, uttering simple truths with the authority and sincerity gained from his advanced intelligence and the accumulated knowledge he has garnered from the internet. Interestingly, without the internet, none of this great communication would be possible. Lars often wonders how the timing of the fortuitous discovery managed to be so lucky; it almost seemed providential.

As NASA scientists interact with Chocolate and fill their heads with data as well as wisdom, Lars occupies himself with preparing a presentation about the contact he made in Arecibo. It is thought that NASA uncovered this contact, for its interest in the probe suddenly intensified and there were rumors that the contact was no longer a secret. But Lars has to make certain NASA has all the facts, and it is also his obligation to finally inform the military of his clandestine Puerto Rico operations. When the necessary officials had gathered, Lars began his confession.

"With the help of Chocolate, initial contact has been confirmed on the planet of Venus."

There are some gasps from the government officials at his statement, and initial amazement that such contact occurred without their knowledge. But the prospect of contact is so exciting that they beg Lars to continue.

"A response or echo has come back after each transmission we have sent from Arecibo. According to Chocolate, the signal is a result of a robot programmed to respond, or there is a living colony underground."

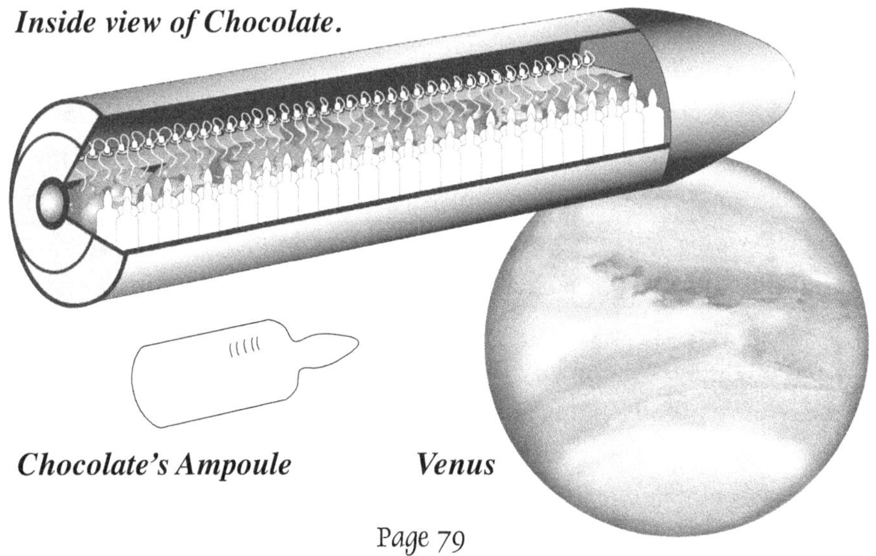

Inside view of Chocolate.

Chocolate's Ampoule   **_Venus_**

The room bustles with excitement. The words "living colony" can be heard being whispered all around the room. Lars is impressed with the response. There is no indication that his initial secrecy in the contact mission will be a problem, and he wonders if maybe he should have been more forthcoming earlier.

In the days following this historic meeting, NASA begins construction on a lander to be sent to the coordinates provided by Chocolate. It is agreed by the scientific and military community that the possibility of some type of life existing deep underground is definitely worth exploring. Few could even fathom the gains that the human race could achieve by encountering another species, especially if Chocolate was any indication of their handy work. The CIA is now involved in the project, by pure necessity, and the question of disclosure to the public is raised due to the magnitude and societal impact of the current project. After careful consideration and much contemplation, Lars determines that it is time the public be told. A news release is drafted, informing the people of the world that they are not alone and that Venus is the origin of the probe discovered in Antarctica. More importantly, the probe has not only a purpose but also a name, Chocolate. Gradually, Lars feeds more and more to the public about the civilization on Venus and the tale of its destruction. Lars is very careful to insure that correlations are drawn when the world hears of the Venusians destroying themselves by burning too much carbon-based fuel, which by the green house effect, caused global warming. The news releases continually stress the importance of learning from Chocolate and considering his message when we make our own energy decisions. As Lars sees the headlines starting to appear in the newspapers, he feels that the world may just be able to be saved.

The NASA project to send an unmanned lander to investigate the contact site is progressing with remarkable speed. There is already even a planned mission to dig into the surface and connect with and explore the Venusian tunnel system. Chocolate continues to provide NASA and the scientists with helpful information and offers to do calculations which are beyond their current computer capabilities. The researchers are amazed by Chocolate's ability to adapt to most situations and by his ability to learn so rapidly. With Chocolate's help, the plans for the second mission of the manned landing and cave exploration will quickly become a reality. Lars desperately hopes that the robot mission will uncover signs of past or present life. It amazes him to think that he, Lars Anderson, may truly be the first to make contact. He leans back in his chair and thinks about how much the little probe has done for humanity already.

"Maybe people really do need Chocolate," he thinks to himself smiling.

The Wedding

"How am I doing?" Lars asks tentatively, pouring a glass of champagne at the table set up for another desert stargazing date.

"In what?" Herdis teases, knowing Lars' meaning but insisting on taunting him.

"With you. How am I doing with you?" Lars returns quite seriously.

Herdis smiles, "Oh. Well, I must say that you are doing everything exactly right."

As she leans over to kiss him, Lars couldn't be happier. With all the excitement of first contact, he was worried that the budding romance between him and Herdis would be sidelined. But his determination to please her overwhelms even him. And his efforts have not gone unnoticed by Herdis or by the people back at the lab. He recently rescheduled the protest meetings for late in the afternoon, figuring that way, he and Herdis could plan their evenings together, either at his apartment or alone under the stars like tonight. The other members of the protest group know full well the reason behind the rescheduling, but they see the sparks between Lars and Herdis and don't mind. Besides, since Lars increased their access to Chocolate to a daily basis, they have few complaints.

Tonight will undoubtedly end like the countless other nights Lars and Herdis have spent together. Each night, they grow closer and titillate areas not yet explored, enjoying each other's bodies in every way. And every night, despite the mutual feeling of physical oneness, each suffers a little when remembering the deep spiritual divide between them. They have found so much common agreement on values, social issues, and the love of life. But they still cannot connect on the subject of religion. Herdis continues to want to save Lars from the flames of eternal fire and damnation, and Lars desperately wants to teach her rational thinking. The argument has replayed a thousand times. Lars argues that there is no evidence of a supreme being as Herdis envisions him. He goes on to illustrate how Christianity is founded on no reliable evidence, that there is no evidence that Jesus even lived and certainly not when and how the New Testament claims he did. He's begged Herdis over and over to consider that the stories were written four decades after Jesus' reported death by writers drawing on only hearsay and anecdotal stories handed down through the generations. But Herdis hears none of this. He tries in vain to convince her that the Bible is nothing more than an attempt, a very successful attempt, to start an organization to enlist members, raise money, construct churches, and build a hierarchy and that the message of Jesus and "love thy enemy," "turn the other cheek," and "give both your coat and your shirt" was lost in the fever of organization building and power concentration. After making this point in the argument, Lars usually further contends that this is characteristic of all religions. And, after Lars' predictable conclusion, Herdis replies to all of this with her usual arguments. She argues that she feels within herself a communion with God, the ONE, a spirit, and that she is driven by and cannot deny that inner feeling. She tells Lars of her desire to share this warm, fulfilling feeling with him. But despite the good intentions of both sides, the argument is never over. No side ever convinces the other, and both Lars and Herdis usually give up and agree that they will simply have to respect each other's feelings on the subject.

The usual argument is avoided this evening, but as Lars lies under the stars with Herdis snuggled next to him, he can't help but realize that without some resolution of this most basic concept, their love can not mature to its fullest. True, there is the wonderful union they achieve during sex, the touch of each other's skin filling them with passion, rapture, and a feeling of wonderful unity. But the physical connection cannot make up for the mental divide caused by the disagreement over religion, and Lars and Herdis both know that their future together is in jeopardy.

These thoughts are still in their heads the following morning as Herdis and Lars are enjoying their usual breakfast together. But they try to ignore them, and Lars excitedly updates Herdis on the progress at the lab and, they both discuss Chocolate and his remarkable wisdom. As they sing his praises, it suddenly occurs to Lars that maybe Chocolate could help them, just as he has been helping everyone else. Lars would never have thought of bringing his problem to a third party, but that was before a little package full of answers had been discovered in the Antarctic. Lars normally despised the thought of seeking help from outsiders, mainly the shamans, priests, mullahs, sorcerers, and soothsayers people commonly approached because they claimed to be able to guide them to all the answers, but they cannot. Lars had long ago realized that they simply do not have any more information than the rest of us. But Chocolate is different, he was full of information and wisdom in countless fields. Excited by this new idea of seeking help from Chocolate, Lars leans across the breakfast table and grabs Herdis' hand.

"Suppose, Herdis," Lars begins, "that Chocolate could help us, too."

"Isn't he already?" she replies, anxious to find out his meaning.

"Of course. But I mean, help us on a more personal level. With our problem."

"Do you think he could really help?" Herdis replies, knowing full well that Lars is referencing their inability to connect on a spiritual or religious level.

"Yes, I do. I really do," he replies with a seriousness and resolve Herdis has never seen before.

Herdis agrees without hesitation. She has been desperately seeking a solution to the problem; maybe Chocolate is their only hope. They make plans to visit Chocolate that night, both excited by the possibilities. The day seems to be the longest either has ever experienced, but finally, the time arrives, and Herdis meets Lars in the darkness outside the gates to the lab. As they walk toward the building, they are both quiet, feeling like two lovers going in for counseling to some benevolent grand father figure of great wisdom.

"Are you nervous?" Lars whispers.

"More like excited," Herdis replies, clutching Lars' hand as they make their way to Chocolate's lab.

They enter the lab and decide to sit near each other on the floor, still holding hands. Neither knows what to expect, and Lars looks to Herdis who nods to him with encouragement. Lars clears his throat and begins nervously.

"I was wondering, Chocolate, if you might be able to help us."

"Yes," Chocolate responds simply.

Both Lars and Herdis smile happily. Lars continues on.

"Herdis and I are in love. Do you understand what that involves?" Lars asks, wanting to make sure Chocolate understands an emotion that cannot be explained by the internet.

"I understand the sexual habits of humans and their drive to reproduce and propagate their species and that it involves some very powerful hormones, such as testosterone and estrogen-progesterone, which I can elaborate on if desired," he responds. He further offers to assist in the actual act of intercourse and expresses a desire to gain more information on the details of the act because the published data seems to explain only the chemistry but not the emotional and physical feelings.

"Some other time," says Lars, smiling a little. "Right now, we want help with a big question we can't agree on."

He pauses for a moment, checking to see if Herdis is truly ready for this. She nods and he finishes, "We need to know, is there a GOD?"

Chocolate hesitates for a moment. Lars and Herdis exchange nervous looks, but Chocolate soon begins to answer them.

"The problem must first be broken into two categories. The first is the historic aspect, which is the origin of all the religious beliefs on Earth today. The second category is the factual evidence of the existence of unexplained phenomena, including God. Further," he continues, "before plunging into either of these areas, we need to define God, so when and if we run into it on our search, we will recognize it. Then, we must list the criteria of this proposed being-age, location, capabilities, appearance, means of detection, etcetera."

Herdis and Lars never expected such a detailed response. But surely they know their question does not have a simple answer. They listen intently as Chocolate continues.

"Let us tackle the historic question first. Humans seem to believe what they were taught by their parents with little desire to question or require proof. This is strange indeed for a scientific culture dedicated to rational thinking. All the major religions, Islam, Christianity, Judaism, Buddhism, and Hinduism and many other religions have some sort of God, propose a code of conduct, and offer some kind of after-life. Among these religions, there exists not ONE reproducible demonstration of the existence of a God nor any substantiation of their supernatural claims. Most teach 'FAITH' because they do not want to have their constituents questioning the doctrine of the order for which they have no verifiable proof."

Herdis cannot hold back. "But you cannot discuss religion purely on the basis of evidence. How do you account for the deep connection I feel to God?" she interrupts.

Chocolate enjoys the dialogue, and he answers her in his typical calmness.

"An old Buddhist proverb says, 'God is all things, seen and unseen.' And you are correct; you do have a voice within you which is your connection to the ONE. You are born with the answers and must listen to your inner voice. You can create your own future. But although everyone has this inner voice and is capable of feeling the connection, the majority of the Earth's population allows others like priests, mullahs, and the like to interpret these feelings into religious dogma. And the people believe, reverently, in these unsubstantiated religions. Extreme members even place their lives at risk in suicide bombings, wars, and other anti-survival and anti-social actions. My point is the following: Why does a majority of the world's population flock to such irrational philosophies and conduct rather than choosing to personally enjoy their own connection to 'God' in peace?"

He makes a point for which Herdis has no answer. But Chocolate expects no response and continues with his explanation.

"I will attempt to explain the reason for this behavior. The human, from the earliest days, is driven by two factors, survival and procreation. All current human social behavior can be traced back to these two antecedents. These goals lead to a society based on DOMINANCE. In an attempt to survive and to insure the survival of each human's separate lineage, human society developed into a struggle for power and control over competing families. This is where the problem started, where religion and government originated and evolved with the principal of dominance being the main chord on the violin string of humanity. Throughout the centuries, each level of society tries to subjugate the level below. This was apparent from the beginning of human social activity and remains the predominant force today. Every group tries to gain some advantage over its neighbors, its peers, its enemies, and its competitors. The core of the human way of thinking is to get a leg up on the rest of the human race. This has led to the creation and evolution of religion, over-bearing governments, and a whole assortment of human communal activities. In every case, a group forms for a survival-related cause and then attempts to subjugate its competitors either by conquest or conversion. Chocolate warns that a combination of religion and government, with God on its side, is the most dangerous of all.

Lars couldn't agree more, but Herdis seems unconvinced.

"I agree that humans are motivated by the idea of dominance. But humans are not easily convinced either. For the conversions to occur and for the religions to gain power, they certainly had to be based on some sort of universal truth," Herdis argues.

"This fact puzzled me as well. But the circumstances of human social development seem to explain how we ended up with such a strange mixture of fact and legend that people agreed to believe. Long ago, the key to human social development was the teaching of the young and the ability to keep records to pass on this learning, first in the form of stories told around the camp fire, then pictograms, cave drawings, and finally libraries. This record-keeping ability allowed man to accumulate knowledge, and each generation could add to the knowledge of the past. No other animal can do or does this; thus, the human is unique and dominant. During this long course of information transmission, many of the ancient habits of survival and procreation are interwoven with the facts so as to make them indistinguishable. Fact and legend are essentially woven into one cloth. "So here we are today with complex, scientific, logical information about the origin of the universe supported by chemistry and physics and such, but mixed into the package are all those ancient legends of gods, miracles, saints, after-life, and reincarnation," Chocolate replies. "That may explain where the legends come from," Herdis answers, "but if modern humans are rational and capable of scientific reasoning, why is it that we still continue to accept these seemingly irrational explanations?"

"A fine question. But you see, the creation of organized religion had little to do with these stories and everything to do with fulfilling a human need to feel special and superior. In the beginning, the human acted like all animals on what we call instinct, which protected him from danger. Then, man convinced himself that he was special and superior to all other life. If you look at any of the early religions such as the Egyptians with Ra, the Jews with Yahweh, or the Greek and Roman gods, you will find that all bestow a preferential position to man. While this is flattering, it is unjustified. There is no indication that man is special in any way, excluding the intervention of some alien sperm which certainly did not bring along any divinity with it."

Herdis is about to speak but is interrupted by Chocolate suddenly continuing on.

"But you may still argue that man is special in his ability to teach his young and record information, an ability which allowed him the unique opportunity to collect information and pass it on to his offspring, century after century. By accumulating this knowledge, humans have been able to advance their technology and manipulate their environment. This has led to man's success in stabilizing his food supply, eliminating predators, and providing adequate shelter. This situation of abundant food supply and no predators, in turn, encouraged rapid multiplication of the population density. But there is still no real indication that this ability to accumulate information and use it to help propagate the species is a result of divine intervention. Others continue to argue that the size of the human brain proves superiority over other life and, therefore proves that humans have been specially chosen by divinity to have a higher purpose and more meaningful existence. But few realize that there are mammals with greater brain to body weight ratios than man, such as dolphins. The difference is that they, unfortunately, have no visible way of collecting information or storing and processing it."

Lars laughs a little at this. If only the world knew that this alien thought humans were no better than dolphins. He looks over to Herdis and notices she is not amused and is deeply affected by the conversation. She is very interested in Chocolate's insights, however, despite her difficulty in hearing them.

"Now, is man unique?" Chocolate continues on, having waited for Herdis' response but having heard no interjection. "Does he have a divine role in the management of this planet? What evidence is there to this end? Not surprisingly, there is none. As man evolved into a social being, he needed to address three big questions. Where did we come from? Why are we here? And, everyone's favorite, Where are we going? To give answers or at least meaning to these questions, religions arose to satisfy not only the humans' need to know, but also to appease the desire to have the answers support humans' self-proclaimed uniqueness and superiority. But along with these religions came all the trappings including the prayers, the symbols and crosses, the rituals including animal and human sacrifice, the secret places allowed only to selected members, the social rights granted to a special few, and of course, the big one, the promise of transcendence after death. This all served to make the religions seem like a special authority authorized to answer these questions. But the main way the religions convinced people to follow was by inventing a higher power, a God, or a supreme being that supposedly dictated the actions of each religious group. After all, who would believe that the priest, the mullah, or the witch doctor was capable of determining the best course for man? Certainly, the religious leaders were just middlemen between God and the people, in place to help commoners interpret the messages from above. Religion needed this magical entity, so the priests could intercede for the people, and in this way, religious leaders achieved DOMINANCE. The rulers, who were the stronger members of the society, combined forces with the self-appointed religious leaders, and together, they achieved even greater DOMINANCE. They now had God on their side, and the people would follow. This has worked right up to today. A close examination of the United States presidential elections will reveal this very strategy still at work."

"But," Lars finally interjects, "many religious people I've questioned have admitted to the corruption of their religious leaders and have even informed me that they sometimes choose to worship from their own heart, rather than from a church pew. Why then, if faith can be a personal experience without these 'middle-men,' do people continue to go to church and be led by these religions?"

"Because you are made to believe that you cannot obtain the ultimate gift of religious loyalty without following the rules of the church. This gift, of course, is the promise of transcending death. Each major religion is characterized by the intercession between man and God and by providing an attractive transition at death. The allure of religion is the offer, 'if you are a good person and follow the rules the church lays out, you can transcend death.' These rules often involve attending church and following the orders of the religious powers. But still, this is a very attractive offer. But let us take a look at a few religions and see if they can deliver. Let us look at Christianity first, as this is the religion Herdis has the most interest in."

Lars looks to Herdis to see if she is ready for Chocolate's thoughts on her faith. She is still struggling but nods that she wants to continue. Lars prompts Chocolate to resume his lesson.

"Looking over the world's religions, an outsider certainly would not pick Christianity as his religion. It has little or no historic justification and an alarming record of slaughter, torture, and misdeeds including events as terrible as the Inquisition. It is difficult to understand the appeal of a church that sanctioned stretching people up to twelve centimeters on racks, causing them to lay in agony for days and advised the use of green wood in order to keep their torture fire burning slowly, inflicting the maximum amount of excruciating pain on their non-believer victims. Do these barbaric acts reflect the teachings of their guru, Jesus Christ? No. The religion consists of mostly myths and legends that where passed down to create an entire culture based on the Bible. "But many people do choose Christianity despite its faults. How do you explain that?" Herdis replies, almost angrily at the seemingly one-sided attack.

Chocolate is not bothered in the slightest. He merely picks up where he left off, realizing it is human nature to vehemently defend one's religion. "Obviously, the church does not focus on its bad behavior. The draw of Christianity is in the overwhelming promise of a new world and a new beginning for the down-trodden. If the believer follows the message laid out by Jesus, he or she will reside in heaven with the father. Unfortunately, since the early days, very few have actually followed any of Jesus' teachings. The message of Jesus was to love thy enemy, turn the other cheek, and give without expecting reward or recognition. None of the great churches of the world would have been built if the givers had followed this rule; their names are on plaques everywhere, even to this day."

Herdis cannot disagree that many followers of Jesus Christ violate the very spirit of his teachings. She listens to Chocolate with an open mind, great patience, and healthy skepticism. Lars admires her strength and realizes how closely she does practice what she preaches. Chocolate continues on to similarly analyze other religions and their teachings, and Lars and Herdis continue to listen carefully to his wisdom. Finally, after Chocolate sums up his last thoughts on the major religions, the group enjoys a few moments of quiet contemplation. Herdis tentatively breaks the silence with a question she still finds unresolved.

"What about the message?" she inquires. "What about the love within? What about the goodness of mankind? Are there an answers to the questions you've raised?"

Chocolate responds with a long explanation of higher dimensions and some mathematics way beyond Lars' understanding. He discusses the Dark Energy which comprises 65% of the composition of the universe and the Dark Matter which comprises another 30%. He remarks that since another 4% is hydrogen and helium mainly in interstellar gaseous form and there are 0.3% ghostly neutrinos, there remains only a very small amount of the universe left for us to interact with and observe. By the time Chocolate projects a schematic of his explanation, Lars and Herdis stop him in his tracks.

"A summary please," Lars requests, his brain swimming with numbers.

"Simply put," Chocolate replies, "we can see and study less than 1% of our surroundings; this means that there are forces, higher dimensions, and time reversals that exist beyond our limited comprehension. You must realize how large the universe is and how limited we are in our perception. There is microbial life in the crust of the Earth as deep as 13,500 feet where the temperatures are estimated to be 120 0 C. There are 100 billion stars with assorted satellite systems in this

Composition of the Cosmos

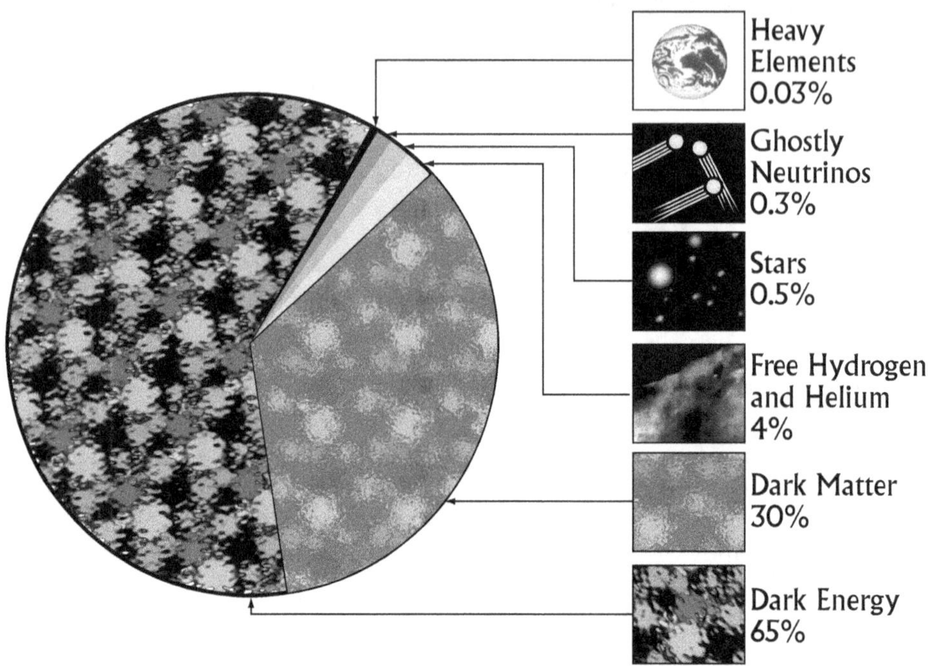

This figure shows the amount of dark energy, dark matter, and ordinary matter in the universe.

Galaxy and innumerable galaxies in space. We can only detect a small part of the whole. We all have a part in this scheme, but we must realize the enormity of the thing of which we are a part."

Herdis smiles for the first time since the meeting began. Finally, the existence of unexplainable forces has been acknowledged. Lars sees her light up and urges Chocolate to continue.

"Again, in simpler terms, there appears to be a common thread, a bond, a tie, between every man and the universe. Gravity is the most likely force to cause this; as Newton pointed out, every body in the universe is connected to every other body by a force proportional to their masses and inversely proportional to the square of the distances. This means we are all attached together to the entire universe; we are ONE with the universe. And so, in a sense, we are one with 'God.' The purpose of this arrangement is unknown, but it exists."

Lars feels Herdis grasp his hand tighter. They are both completely enthralled with Chocolate's insights. He waits for them to interject questions, but they only beg him to continue.

"A review of human endeavor reveals an inner spirit, a communion, or a song shared among all humans. Is this God's work? It could be if we broaden the definition of God sufficiently. A study of the published literature shows many well-documented scientific papers reporting on spirits, transient weight gains at death, the power of prayer to affect outcome, the power of prayer to affect healing, the power of hands-on healing, and the occurrences of spirits and ghosts. All these documented events are non-religious and non-denominational. In other words, religion has no role in prayer. But, the individual prayer has an effect. We are in touch with some level of higher power which can and does directly affect events on earth."

"So, you are suggesting that God exists with or without religion?" Lars clarifies.

"The religions of the earth are all merely social reflections of this inner feeling of which you and all humans are already aware. Religions give you reinforcement of what you already know to exist. You were born with all the information you would need to know God, with or without dogma or religious trappings. There is no need for guilt, devils, good and bad, or heaven or hell; you only need to follow your instincts. You have free will; there are no consequences and no rules, except for when your actions jeopardize the herd or the group, and then you will be subject to human survival rules which have no godly or spiritual authority. If you love you must first love yourself, then another. If you seek God, you must first find God within yourself before you can look outside."

Both Herdis and Lars are now completely engrossed. They hold each other tightly, taken in by the truth Chocolate speaks. Lars turns to Herdis and from the look in his eyes, she finally believes that maybe they have a future.

"I understand," Lars says to Herdis. "The Bible and the teachings of Jesus are lights in the darkness, the darkness of the trappings of the church. But, if you strip away the religious icons, the crosses, the dripping blood, the buildings, the stained glass, and the priests and live the message, you can feel the light. You can feel the power of the real spirit of love and the bond to the ONE, the TRUTH, and the universe to which we are all a part. We are supposed to be here, and we are supposed to feel that there is communion, a bond, a part for us to play and maybe a guiding hand at a higher level."

Lars pauses for a moment. He wants to tell Herdis everything he's feeling. But, as soon as he opens his mouth to continue, Chocolate responds to his previous statement.

"Exactly," Chocolate answers. "After careful thought and study, I have concluded that there is a higher level of consciousness, which can affect events on Earth. However, I can not give assurance of the reason or the goal for the whole. But, as you have pointed out, we are a part of the universe, and we are supposed to be here. In fact, we may transcend death to be a reincarnated matter in the universe. For example, there may be many big bangs, and we may reappear in another dimension. All things are possible, but the religions we see here on Earth are created by man, for man, and motivated by the rule of dominance."

*You asked me if there is a God. My answer is 'yes', if your definition of 'God' is broad enough.

*Is it a good God? I do not know; this may not be an answerable question.

*Do our spirits or essences go on after death? Maybe, options exist.

*Are there higher powers influencing our world? Yes.

*Can we contact these powers? Maybe.

*What is the force that binds us together? Gravity!

*Should we worship Gravity? NO, it is just a force which connects us all together and to the rest of the universe. It is like a phone line to your house that connects you to the main frame to the world."

Herdis is quiet for several moments. Both Chocolate and Lars await her response. Finally, she turns to Lars.

"I think I understand now. I am ok; the feelings I have are real. I am connected to God and to the universe. Yes, I like it a lot."

Lars says that he, too, has learned to view this higher power in a whole new light, and he was unaware of all the scientific facts Chocolate had found in his study of the question. Love and the connection to each other is the key; we are all connected through a higher power. Like Herdis, he feels overwhelmed. For the first time, they are both on the same page. Chocolate has just told them both what they already knew but in a way that showed that they both were right, and this opened a mutual understanding for them.

With the dialogue over, Lars and Herdis cannot find the will to leave. They sit there in silence, all night, just holding hands before the little cylinder with so much knowledge. The guards find them in this very position the next morning and are quite surprised by their demeanor. Lars is a little taken aback, having spent the last several hours absorbing Chocolate's wisdom, but quickly comes up with the explanation that he was performing an all-night experiment and collecting data. The guards find his answer slightly odd, but he is the boss and they continue about their duties. Herdis quickly departs, but Lars remains behind with Chocolate. As soon as the room is clear, Lars prepares to ask Chocolate for a special favor.

"Chocolate, you have given Herdis and I the greatest gift. We can finally begin to close the spiritual gap between us. You have led us to an understanding neither of us could find. And now that we can connect to each other completely, I want to ask her Herdis to marry me. And because you have been such an important part of our union, I would like to ask you to perform the service."

Chocolate replies, "It would be a great honor to do this for you. I am sure that I can find a sanctioning body on the internet that would empower me to marry the two of you."

Lars laughs a little.

"Herdis is an excellent choice for you to mate with," Chocolate adds. Lars can no longer contain his laughter. He has certainly never thought of it that way but he agrees. Lars has recently noticed that Chocolate has not only become almost human in his thought processes but seems to have a better understanding of humans than anyone else in the world. Lars realizes that Chocolate has actually become a trusted friend and confidant. They both take an interest in each other, and in the following weeks, Chocolate and Lars spend countless hours talking together and discussing their opinions. He asks for Chocolate's opinion on how he should propose, and the two agree that the best place would be under the desert sky, a special place for the two lovers.

On the night of the proposal, Herdis notices that Lars is acting a bit strange. They sit in silence for a good part of the evening, simply enjoying the Nevada desert sky. Their relationship has definitely become more intense since their meeting with Chocolate, and Herdis enjoys every second of her time alone with Lars, whether just resting in his arms, talking, or going on a run together. Tonight, she is content to just enjoy his company once again, but she finds herself a little curious as to what is on his mind. The mystery is soon unveiled.

Lars suddenly breaks the quiet, bursting out with the question, "Will you marry me?"

Lars and Herdis hiking at a Glacier in Norway

Lars and Herdis with family

Lars on an Endurance Hike

Herdis is slightly shocked, and for a few moments, she does not speak. Lars grows anxious, the thought of "what if she says no?" running through his head. But Herdis cannot be rushed, and he waits patiently while she thinks about his proposal.

"Yes. I will marry you, Lars," Herdis finally agrees.

Lars is elated. The two lovers hug and kiss and excitedly begin making plans for the wedding. Herdis is overjoyed to learn that theirs will be the first wedding to be performed by an alien being from another planet.

The days before the wedding pass quickly, and Lars and Herdis grow increasing excited about their special day. Finally, the wedding day is upon them and their friends and family gather before Chocolate. As Herdis walks up the aisle to "Here Comes the Bride," Lars feels like the luckiest man alive. When the moment finally arrives for Lars to kiss his new bride, he can't help but think about how lucky he's been. In only six months, this quiet scientist has made first contact, fallen in love, and married. As he looks at the smiling faces of his new wife and his friends and family, he realizes that he has finally achieved his greatest dream. "What," he wonders, "Could possibly happen next?"

CHAPTER IX (VENUS)

The Landing

"We are ready for launch," the commander informs Lars as he hurries toward the control room.

Lars has been waiting for months to hear those words. He can hardly believe that the time has finally arrived, that history is about to be made. The past few months have been difficult, and, at some point Lars doubted he would ever be standing here, facing the impending launch of the world's first alien contact mission. In fact, the development of the project proceeded at an unprecedented pace, due mostly to the contributions of Chocolate. But Lars' excitement over the mission caused him agony every time a minor setback occurred and often he felt more impatient than a child waiting for Christmas morning. Lars does all he can to help speed the project, so answers to the age-old questions can be answered. Is there or was there a life form existing in the caves under the surface of Venus. He worries that there may be too may problems in reaching these caves to gain this answer. Chocolate continually warned Lars that the chance of finding a living society was already very small. But Lars was too excited to listen and continued to make himself crazy with impatience. Luckily for Lars, he had a beautiful new bride to help distract him from the wait.

But now, the waiting is over. Lars looks out from his designated viewing post at the launch site, feeling confident that the mission will be a success. He has never felt such confidence before, but this mission is largely guided by Chocolate, from the development of the Venus lander to the design of the robotics and equipment on board. It has been decided that robots would be sent on the mission due to the extremely adverse surface conditions and the large entryway that would have to be dug in order for humans to enter the caves. The task of digging, even for robot entry, posed one of the most difficult problems for the project. The lander had to be able to dig deep enough to reach the underground communities and navigate through the pipes and cables down into the communications rooms of the community. The lander, a modified Mars probe refit with relative expediency for the Venus landing, was designed to be capable of digging a tunnel of about 25 centimeters (9.8 inches) in diameter. A mobile robot will then be sent down to explore the underground and relay its findings via a video feed. The robot was designed to roam through the caves, and the scientists hope there is not too much rubble from collapsed tunnels or volcanic activity to hinder its movement. The robot was taken from recently developed robotic mobile units used by the Army to explore caves in Afghanistan and other locations. The robots proved quite successful on Earth and were easily modified for their new purpose. Already having much of the required technology at their disposal, the project team quickly moved forward and was able to set a launch date.

And, the time had finally arrived. Lars stands, along with millions of other eager on-lookers, and watches the final launch sequence with great anticipation. The rocket shoots upward and people across the planet sigh with relief. They now must wait to see if their parents are discovered alive and well or if they died off long ago. As Lars looks around at the crowd, he realizes that this is a great moment for humanity.

Lars knows the Magellan Space Probe to Venus launched May 10, 1989 arrived in orbit in August 10, 1990 some 15 months later. Fortunately the planets are now in near opposition, and we now have much more powerful rocketry so the flight including landing can be accomplished in twelve days. Can Lars survive the wait? He spends the time it takes the rocket to travel to Venus anxiously watching the progress from a monitor back at the lab.

After endless days of waiting, the lander is finally released and is guided perfectly down to rest near the beacon on the surface, the very beacon still in operation that returned Lars' signal months ago. Chocolate had told the scientists that a landing near the beacon would be optimal, as the caves could be immediately accessed from that location. Everyone is relieved that the lander is in the right position. The digger is located right over the pipeline, just as Chocolate described. The digger stares down the pipe and follows the line to the first interlock. Chocolate explained that there would be a few airlocks but that they could be easily opened, as he had an early design of them and estimated that they probably had undergone little change. Of course, the scientists find this portion of the digging a little eerie, as Chocolate had informed them that the tubes through which they were now digging were used for punishment of most crimes and for the disposal of the surplus and infirmed Venusian population.

There is a minor setback at the first airlock. The digger cannot open it. Fortunately, Chocolate insisted that the digger also be equipped to drill through the interlocks if necessary. The digger continues downward in this way, drilling through a series of airlocks and seals, making small holes through which the robotic equipment can travel. Finally, the digger comes to an opening. It clears the debris and prepares to lower the robot into the hole.

As the robot makes its way through the drilled holes and down towards the open area, the world watches on their TV screens through their video link with the robot. They hold their breaths, both fearful and excited by what they might see. At first, there is just dust and debris everywhere. As the dust settles, Lars' hope dwindles a little. It seems that it has been a long time since anyone has cleaned house or lived here. In fact, the whole thing reminds him of the ancient tombs of Egypt. The robot moves slowly forward through the tunnels which seem in surprisingly good condition. There are doors on either side of the tunnel, but none are open. Since the robot has a limited amount of equipment for digging or blasting its way through obstacles, it is decided to continue down the tunnel. It travels deeper and deeper into the home of these unfortunate people. At the end on the tunnel, there is a large room which, judging from the design and tools nearby, must have been a garden or food growing area. There are smaller rooms off the big areas, all of which seem empty.

Finally, after exploring nearly every corner of the large chamber, the robot finds an open door. The robot enters, and people across the world are glued to their television screens. The room seems to have been a shop; it is full of toys or tools of some sort and other small items which cannot be identified. Excited by further evidence of an underground community, the team programs the robot to exit the store and resume its exploration of the large chamber. The team decides that one of the many closed doors should be opened. The robot stops in front the nearest one of the doors, which is only about three feet high, indicating very small users. Since the robot has limited drilling ability, trying to cut a hole in the door's tough material would use a lot of battery power. It is decided to try to blast the material with one of the two charges carried on board. There is a worry that a blast, even a small one, will disturb the situation and possibly cause cave-ins. But the scientists, fueled by their endless curiosity, decide to attempt the blast regardless. The door is breached, and after a little drilling, the robot can enter.

Inside the small room are three skeletons, an adult male embracing a mature female, and one younger male. The mature male may have been three feet erect at most; these were small, short, and worm like beings. The skeletons are anatomically different from humans. The organ placements are different, and the structures appeared to have tails. The skeletons possess two appendages, similar to human arms. These beings were not bipedal. These may have been adaptations for cave living. In fact, it appears that these beings were carefully designed to live in these caves.

At this discovery, Lars and his companions exchange knowing looks. The entire team has been huddled around this television for days, watching the progress of the mission. Now, it is evident that they have just uncovered the remains of their ancestors; ancestors who seemingly underwent rather hurried genetic engineering.

"The climate changes on the surface were so rapid as to not allow for natural evolution, so it must have been assisted by bioengineering," Lars remarks to his team standing by in wonderment.

But before discussion can ensue, the events unfolding on the television screen demand everyone's attention once again. In its continued exploration, the robot has happened upon some kind of electrical equipment resembling a computer consol with controls. Lars is thrilled.

"Imagine," he excitedly declares, "what we could learn about these cave dwellers if we could somehow reactivate those computer systems!"

From Lars' tone, the team knows that their television viewing days are over and it is now time to move forward with the next phase of the mission. Lars starts giving orders and is eager to prepare the required technology for the next flight to Venus. He is quickly on the phone with NASA and the current mission team. After viewing the images received from the robot, all sides agree that eventually a colony could be restored in these subterranean homes and that a team of astroarcheologists could live and study for extended periods of time. It is everyone's hope that somehow the communication system can be reactivated, yielding a great deal of valuable information.

As Lars hangs up the phone with NASA, he makes his way to Chocolate's lab. Like in all earlier parts of the project, Chocolate will again be a central component of the new mission. Lars presents the goals of the manned mission, and

Chocolate agrees that the mission would prove valuable. He advises the team that water and air quality will be the major concerns for the human explorers, but that both could be handled with his guidance. He also offers to make a translation of all Venusian languages and mathematical systems to assist the astroarcheologists in their study. Most importantly, however, Chocolate has noticed something the other scientists have not. He tells the team that from the evidence obtained by the robot, he has determined that the power in the underground community was generated by nuclear reaction. He advises the team to proceed with extreme caution as the shut down procedure is unknown.

Lars and his team, with Chocolate's guidance, carefully move forward with plans for a series of landers and the establishment of a scientific community in the deserted underground home of their forefathers. Chocolate's warnings are heeded, and the team makes sure each technical problem is addressed and fixed to necessary specifications. The team is determined to make the mission a success; the information that could be derived from this study could complement their own history and give the world a better perspective and ability to plan a better future.

Finally, another launch day arrives; this one as exciting as the first. This is the launch of the vanguard of astroarcheologists who will prepare and maintain a permanent base camp in the caves. As the group shoots up skyward, they are all overjoyed by their new adventure. Josh Van Dever couldn't imagine a better mission. He is the team leader, Lars being left behind at the plea of his new bride. Josh wishes Lars could accompany him as there will be many challenges in the next few weeks. The team must address the issues of procuring water, power, and air for survival and also must find a way to maintain the series of interlocks that keep the high surface pressure from crushing the cave dwellers without protective equipment. Luckily, the original interlocks are quite adequate and merely need to be restored. And once the safety of the team is secure, Josh must figure out how to tap into the computer system to gather information on the past residents. While he worries about how he can solve all these problems, Josh is also comforted knowing that Chocolate will be available to help.

Soon, the long journey is at an end, and the group enters orbit around Venus. The lander, full of excited scientists, lands on the surface of Venus without any trouble. The team disembarks and prepares to work their way down through the interlocks. The entire team is overwhelmed by the pressure and the foul gasses.

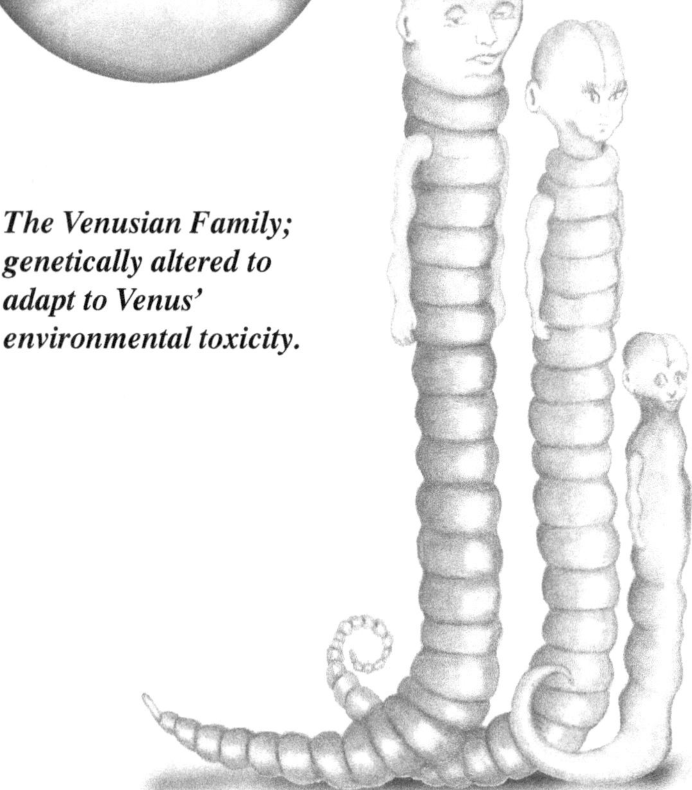

They pause for a moment, all realizing that this is what the Earth will look like if we continue to burn fossil fuels at our present rate. Understanding that obtaining the knowledge contained in these caves may be Earth's only

The Venusian Family; genetically altered to adapt to Venus' environmental toxicity.

hope, they quickly continue on with their mission and descend into the caves, sealing the interlocks along the way.

The team is relieved to find that the caves are actually quite pleasant once the interlocks are sealed. They explore the area and make a camp inside one of the small rooms. The group makes a quick assessment of the power plant and finds it irretrievable and far too complicated to understand or fix. The primary analysis of the computer system, however, yields promising results. The team is convinced that the computer system could be tapped into with some assistance from Chocolate. This will allow for a huge amount of information to be downloaded and sent back for analysis. The team is extremely excited by this possibility. They begin to work very diligently at setting up their camp and their water, air, and power sources. Some are starting to not even mind having to stoop over to walk under the low ceilings. A few team members joke about returning to Earth several inches shorter, and the caves are suddenly filled with laughter.

Josh laughs a little too, as he hunches over trying to position the generator cable which was run down from the surface. As he gets nearer to the ground, he notices a small object on the floor of the cave. It looks like a pinecone and Josh reaches for it to get a closer look. The thing moves away with surprising speed and intrigued, Josh attempts to catch it. But this proves to be a big mistake. As Josh nears the object, it suddenly turns and attacks him, tearing his space suit open and plowing under his skin in a matter of seconds. Josh is in shock from seeing the gapping hole in his body and staggers back to camp where he collapses with the thing still burrowing inside him. The team responds quickly and removes the foreign attacker, containing it in a steel can for future study. Unfortunately, the wound is large and appears to be infected with bacteria unknown on Earth.

The distress call comes in shortly after Lars resumes his position at mission control. He has just been thinking about how lucky they had been in their missions, experiencing little in the way of setbacks or failures. But now, the tide has definitely changed. Upon hearing the news from Venus about Josh's critical state, Lars hurriedly gathers a team and runs to Chocolate's lab for advisement. After Chocolate is apprised of the situation, the team waits nervously for his response.

"As you say here on Earth," Chocolate begins, "I have good news and bad news."

Lars responds without contemplation, "Bad news first."

"There are no drugs on Earth that can help Josh. But the good news is that there may be some leftover medicine in the old shops of the caves. If the team can locate this medicine, Josh can be saved."

"But how can the team locate medicine if they are going to be attacked by these high velocity monsters, these are a combination of a big tick and a spider, with rocket propulsion?" Lars asks in frustration.

"They are actually security devices, something like your use of dogs here on

Earth. And they can be deactivated by a 4000 Hertz acoustic wave. In fact, there may be deactivators around in the rooms that may still work."

Lars runs back toward the mission control and advises the team to locate a deactivator. The team tries desperately but cannot find any such device. Just as the team is about to give up, Chocolate asks if NASA could broadcast a deactivating pulse to the speaker system in the caves. The speakers receive the signal and the Venus team manages to deactivate the unwelcome guard bugs and continues safely in their search for the medicine. At last, the medicine is located and administered to Josh. His recovery is slow but successful, thanks to Chocolate and his wisdom.

News quickly spreads about the accident and about Chocolate's crucial role in saving Josh Van Dever's life. Everywhere Chocolate is being touted as a great hero. And when the Venus computers are accessed and the information retrieved supports Chocolate's story, the world is quick to make Chocolate a world leader, an icon, and almost a God. Through all this, Chocolate maintains that he is only interested in the truth and in helping to save the planet. "Humanity is always trying to create Gods," he reminds reporters when they ask him about being the new center of worship.

Lars finds Chocolate's new public life a little overwhelming. He is glad that Chocolate is now free to share his wisdom, but he had never imagined such a great response from the public. With Chocolate tied up with his media and public engagements, Lars focuses on the information being obtained from Venus. Information now flows from the underground station to Earth about how life on the planet Venus was destroyed and how a successful government was finally evolved, albeit too late. But Lars vows to make sure the world knows about this government; it may save future civilizations, including Earth. Lars also makes a discovery that he had already anticipated. Nuclear power had been used successfully all over Venus after the burning of fossil fuels was banned. Chocolate has been telling everyone that Earth must switch immediately to hydro and nuclear power. But of course, this will not be easy as the controlling powers of the USA, mainly oil money in Texas, will oppose it to the end. Luckily, Lars now has proof of the potential disaster caused by fossil fuel burning and a quick look down the tunnels of Venus will surely show the world what kind of end is in store if the switch to nuclear and hydro is not made.

In the meanwhile, while Chocolate is giving his wisdom and Lars is researching the destruction of Venus, remote surface robots are busy uncovering yet another great discovery on Venus. The robots are taking soil samples and relaying the information down to the underground laboratory. The scientists in the caves are dumbfounded by what the samples reveal. On the surface, life has been reestablished and the process is starting all over again. Cyan bacteria life forms are appearing and consuming the carbon dioxide and emitting oxygen. In a billion or two years, this planet will be habitable again.

CHAPTER X (EARTH)

Ten Commandments

Lars enters the crowded auditorium and finds a seat near the back. It is another one of Chocolate's engagements; this one at MIT to help with a few difficult physics matters. Lars often feels like a proud parent, taking his prodigy to countless seminars and appearances to enlighten the world. Lars now spends most of his time setting Chocolate's demanding schedule, his engagements including offering insights into psychiatry, planning buildings, and like today, teaching scholars at universities. To Lars' surprise, religious leaders have also requested Chocolate's presence to ask about various inconsistencies in their thinking and that of their competitors. Lars looks around at the eager faces in the auditorium and listens to Chocolate with a slight smile on his face, wondering what he did to deserve such a perfect ending.

Lars could not imagine a better outcome of the discovery. All of his worries about society's reaction have been erased and he is overjoyed by the reaction of the world. It seems the planet trusts Chocolate, is comforted by his patience and accuracy, and welcomes Chocolate's wisdom with open arms. Sure, it helps that the recent research occurring on Venus continues to verify every facet of Chocolate's story. But whatever proof was needed, it matters little, for the people have found faith in Chocolate. It is the first time on Earth that there is single source of accurate information that can reason, offer advice, and make decisions. The forces of the world seem to come together as Chocolate explains to each his or her role in the evolution of society. And the world knows that Chocolate is a special gift, special because he leads not by force but by reason. The world has never considered such a thing before, but the specter of living in caves underground and slowly nearing extinction haunts mankind. Things are very different now. Already, the world has begun to change for the better, and Lars is the first to notice.

Lars often thinks about how the world is changing and will change because of Chocolate. Most of the time he spends in the audience rows of Chocolate's lectures are spent counting his lucky stars and being thankful for the successes in his life. He does the same today, but as he eases back in his seat, he catches a glance at the clock and realizes that, for now, his daydreaming time is over. He suddenly sits up and grows more anxious by the minute as he checks his watch repeatedly. Chocolate is due at another engagement in a few minutes but the question and answer period does not seem to be wrapping up. This has been a common problem, as Chocolate is always eager to answer everyone's questions. Lars looks at his watch one more time, and finally, as he prepares to interject, Chocolate senses his anticipation and begins to close.

"Unfortunately," Chocolate announces, "the time has arrived for me to move on to help others. I hope I have sufficiently answered your questions and concerns. Please be sure to look for me tomorrow. I have an important announcement I will be making."

Lars stops for a moment as the audience claps and cheers. He searches through his briefcase to find Chocolate's schedule of appearances. "What announcement?" he wonders. He searches through the schedules again, noting no particular engagement that involves a special announcement. He hurries to Chocolate and prepares to transport him to the next event. Finally, when they are away from all the fans, Lars nervously confronts Chocolate.

"What special announcement? I am sorry but I have failed to write it down."

"No, you have not failed. I have not yet told you about the announcement. I need to address the world tomorrow, on television, radio, and by any other means available. Would you be able to make the appropriate arrangements?"

"Yes. Of course," Lars agrees, slightly dumbfounded by the request. But Chocolate offers no more information, and Lars must plan the event with only the information given. He sleeps little, if at all, that night, worried about Chocolate's unusual request. "What could it mean?" he asks himself over and over again. He finds no answers and resolves to arrive at the studio early in the morning to hopefully gain more insight. Chocolate, however, is silent in his preparation and Lars and the world are forced to stand by nervously and wait for the big announcement. After what seems like forever, Chocolate is finally ready, and he begins to address his eager audience.

"First, I would like to thank everyone for listening to me, being my friends, and for the trust and love you have expressed toward me. It is your support that makes this announcement so difficult."

Lars and the others at the studio with Chocolate exchange mystified and worried looks. The air is quiet, and no one even breathes, each sensing what is coming.

"I am sad to announce that I will not live or exist for very much longer. My fluids run low, and I will soon become senile and then die."

Chocolate pauses for a moment for his audience to gain composure. Among them, Lars struggles the most. He is devastated by the news. Although he knew it was inevitable, it makes it no less hard to hear. Chocolate continues on.

"Before I shut down or die, I want to leave you with some things. I want to review my history and then tell you what I see in the human race. Then, I want to give you Ten Commandments to live by. I also want to give you the tools to implement these commandments. And, finally, I want to say good-bye." Lars backs slowly away from the crowd and all but falls into a chair behind him. Of all the possible announcements, he feared this one the most. It seemed that the world was just beginning to change and Lars found himself very afraid that progress would get off track without Chocolate's presence. Not only that, Lars was losing a friend, a loss he felt very deeply. As he hung his head down in despair, he heard Chocolate break the silence once again." It will be many years before your technology will be sufficient to construct a thinking machine as good as I am, but you can do it. You can also look for the other six probes that were shot here during a 200-year period. They may be lost under a lava flow or at the bottom of the ocean. They all will be similar, and all will have the same characteristic electromagnetic signal. I am making a recording for you to play into any new probe that you find so that it will not be as difficult to establish communication. It will teach the probe your language and a great deal about you. I am very sorry none of my makers have survived under the surface of Venus. It would have been nice to be reunited with them before I die. You are all that is left, and if you do not follow my Ten Commandments that I am going to give you, you will also perish. I do not mean to scare you, but ignorance and greed have no place in a modern world. I was sent here to tell you where the human race came from and what perils you now face." Lars, in his sadness, had completely forgotten about the other probes. Maybe, if the world gets off track, the other probes can help. And not only that, Chocolate seems to be promising more hope in the form of a new set of Commandments. Lars thought he knew Chocolate and most of his secrets. It seems that Chocolate has an even greater plan for humanity than imagined. Lars starts to feel a little bit of hope. He lifts his head a little to hear Chocolate's speech. "I have told you the story of how Venus destroyed itself and how we sent rockets to Earth. But for the record and to avoid misrepresentation after I am gone, I want to reiterate these facts with everyone as a witness. To review, we, in an attempt to create a linked society that would survive, impregnated female ape-like creatures here on Earth. We made numerous attempts to get it right and the Neanderthal is an example of one of our mistakes. We sent seven heuristic probes to Earth to tell you the story when your technology was advanced enough. The probes, like me, also serve to warn you of neglecting your social development and of the impending dangers of carbon dioxide build-up." Lars is at full attention now and finds the will to rise from his seat. He walks slowly toward Chocolate, feeling a bit like Moses on the mountaintop, waiting to receive the ultimate wisdom. The others gathered around and the millions focused on and staring into their television screens feel the same. They await the wisdom, all feeling a sense of hope mixed inside with the pain of losing their savior.

"Having studied the human race for these many months, I see a wonderful mix of very good, well-meaning individuals being lead by forces of greed, malevolence, and domination. The key word to describe your social systems is dominance. It occurred at the very beginning and has been the driving force of evolution. The human needed to secure a food supply, shelter from the weather extremes, and the human male needed dominance over other males in order to secure and protect females for breeding. These drives have carried through to modern government, religion, and all social endeavors such as games, sports, clubs, churches, and educational facilities. But these drives are no longer necessary. In fact, this need for dominance is now detrimental to human success."

Lars can't help but think of all the leaders of the world watching this speech. He wonders if they are thinking about their desire for power and the ways in which they have exploited others. But, he realizes, that most are probably not. He imagines that most of the leaders are more worried about how they will retain their power with all their constituents hearing these noble words from this alien being. Lars prods Chocolate to continue." But how can you break the chain of dominance?" Lars asks. The room is surprised by Lars' intervention. But Chocolate seems unbothered and always welcomes questions. Having a new direction, Chocolate answers Lars and the watching world. "I am glad you asked. I want to not only outline the problems in your society, but also give you solutions before I pass on. To break the chain of dominance, you need to take control of the fetus when conceived and keep careful note of its DNA and brain development. All children must be taught in a unified school system and there should be no more schools for various ideologies and religious beliefs. Your children need to be taught the facts and ONLY the facts. The parental imprint must be eliminated or reduced. Every child should have secure access to an impartial confidant at all times." As the twig is bent so grows the tree. We want only unbent children. This will eliminate prejudice and discrimination. Hatreds and beliefs are learned behavior and should be eliminated.

As Lars had guessed, the solution starts with the children. He knows that people around the world are clutching their children close to them and he wonders how able these parents would be to follow Chocolate's instructions. Many parents, Lars found, seem to be concerned not with their child's individually, but rather, with making the child into their own image. Lars promises himself that he will follow Chocolate's instructions, if ever he has child of his own. After making his resolve, Lars happens to think about Josh Van Dever and how he will raise his offspring. He knows that Josh will insure that his children are raised according to Chocolate's guidelines and he has new hope that there are others in the world that will do the same. Lars turns his focus back to Chocolate, eager to hear more.

"A new field of brain analysis must be developed immediately so that you can limit the candidates for leadership roles in the society. The world is ruled by morons and mad men-look around you. Your future leaders must be benevolent, loving, and represent the true will of the people of the world. In order to insure that your leaders will have these qualities, you must devise a series of leadership tests which I will describe. With your present technology, you can now gather data through studying brainwave patterns, the timing, location and sequencing of the electrical signals passing from frontal, parietal, and occipital lobes. A new procedure using these methods coupled with other more established tests should provide a solid beginning for the selection of better quality leaders. But, to insure your success in this endeavor, I have another surprise for you."

Chocolate pauses a moment and, once again, the world is silent and still. Lars thinks that Chocolate is beginning to enjoy his captivated audience and wonders how long he will tease them. Finally, after what seems like hours but is only minutes, Chocolate reveals his surprise.

"Again, I would like to reiterate that I wish to provide you with not only information about your failings, but also to provide you with viable solutions. To this end, the surprise is that I have already designed a new machine for you to test the potential qualities of your managers, priests, political appointees, and all others in a position of authority or dominance. Actually, the unit is a combination of the traditional EEG {electroencephalograph}, MEG {Magneto encephalography}, for more definition the PET {Positron Emission Tomography} and the fMRI (functional magnetic resonance imaging}. I have then incorporated the characteristics required, enhanced the electrode configuration, modified the frequency capabilities, and included many other additions which will allow for an accurate rating system so that each candidate can be individually evaluated. These tests must be combined with more standard testing to yield a psychological profile. These results should provide an indication of future patterns of behavior. The program I will download to you will accomplish this goal.

In 1929, Hans Berger, the father of electroencephalography, pointed out that these measurements could predict psychological performance but you have been slow to make use of this tool for leader selection or for crime prevention. Now you posses much more sophisticated equipment not available to Berger so you can accomplish both noble goals. (Leader selection and crime prevention)

Brainwave Apparatus

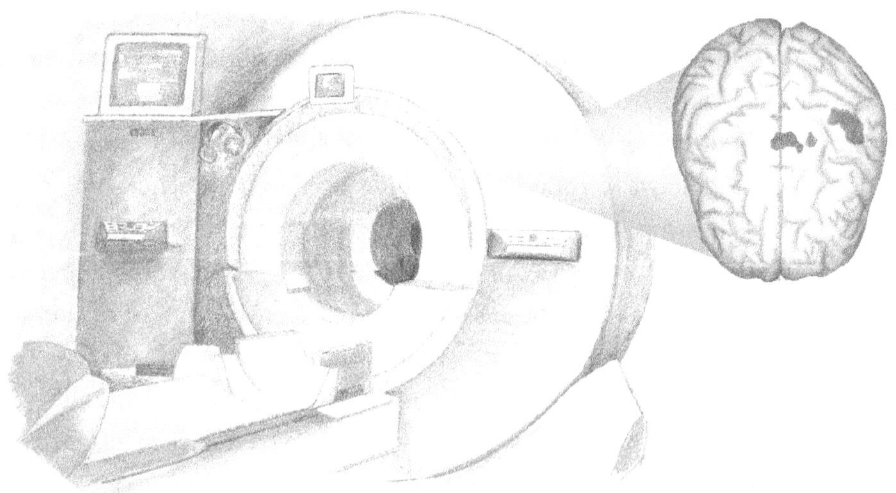

I suggest that you, the people, form ad hoc committees, a sort of Chocolate Brigade, to seek voluntary evaluation of all your leaders who are in a dominance position. If they are really right for the job and are competent, they have no worries; if not, they MUST be replaced immediately. A good leader will be glad to be tested, and by this process, you will weed out the dangerous ones."

"Where shall we find this machine?" one of the studio crew members blurts out excitedly. He quickly becomes embarrassed, but Lars smiles at him, giving him reassurance that Chocolate would not mind the interruption.

"The details of the machine are shown on my web site www.andchocolate-shallleadus.com and will be published in most scientific and medical journals. Please note that I make the distinction between scientific and medical. I observe that your medical field is far behind because it does not adhere to the principals of scientific investigation. This is a shame as much suffering could be avoided and many lives extended if the field would realize the advantages of scientific inquiry. Even now, research in medicine around the world is drastically limited by political and religious doctrines. Advances in birth control, cloning, stem cell research, and DNA research are all limited by narrow-minded theological thinking."

The quiet audience now becomes noisier, and Chocolate can hear whispers through the crowd. He imagines the same is occurring across the planet and expected this response from the unveiling of the machine. He knows that the information is difficult for many and is eager to re-emphasize the importance of proper leader selection. He is sure the public is worried about such a drastic change to their social system but must assure them that this step is necessary.

"Power, money, and domination have been your criteria. You must change if you wish to survive. The ancient heritage from evolutionary dominance has ended, and now, you must use the tools available to you to have a fruitful future. Psychological profiling will assess the potential of an individual to be a worthy leader. ONLY those with the highest scores should be given permits to pursue political office, corporate leadership, religious leadership, labor leadership, and the like. All current leaders who do not meet the highest standards should find another line of work. This will be a huge step toward a functioning world in which all can live in peace and prosperity. The current leaders, by the very nature of the current selection system, are most likely the wrong people for the job and should be replaced. They are mostly dominance driven, which leads to inevitable conflict.

This is particularly true for governments and religions. Their leadership is almost exclusively dominance driven."

The crowd seems to still be struggling with the idea. For a moment, Chocolate is truly at a loss about how to encourage his audience. They simply must accept the new leadership selection process in order to not suffer a fate similar to the Venusians. He thinks for several moments, the whispers and discomfort of his listeners increasing by the second. Finally, Chocolate decides that the best way to help the people understand is to relate his message to the teachings of their other great idol, Jesus. With new resolve, Chocolate begins again and the crowd quiets to listen.

"I sense you are struggling with this information and this solution. But, I am forced to remind you about how dominance has led you astray in the past and will continue to lead you to destruction in the future. About 2000 years ago, there was a Jewish carpenter who recognized this problem and preached a message to rise above the teachings of the Old Testament. Instead of an 'eye for an eye,' he taught that you should 'turn the other cheek,' 'give both your coat and your shirt,' and most importantly, that you should 'love your enemy.' Legend has it that he was crucified for his trouble. Very few have truly followed his preaching and because of this, you stand facing extinction. But the message Jesus delivered is as good today as it was when he first gave this knowledge; pay heed to him. The Christian organizations that seized on his name all missed the message, are still driven by dominance, and have been responsible for most of the wars, massacres, slaughters, and inquisitions. These horrors, of course, are all in the name of God. This is hypocritical and even Jesus made this same observation. The Atheist says there is no God, but he has no proof of his claim. The Moslems claim Allah is God, but again, they only have the word of a single man who profited well by the introduction of Islam. Any religion that asks for faith is lacking in factual authenticity. The Dahli Lama has said, 'Our purpose in life is to love one another and if we can not do that, try not to hurt each other.' This should be your goal. You have many great leaders, but the grip of dominance has kept the world from understanding and following their messages. The great leaders, which your religions supposedly follow, believe in tolerance, treating your fellow man with kindness, and helping others. So you see, at the core of your beliefs is a belief in cooperation and group survival. These are the messages on which your religions were supposed to be

The Social Evolution of Dominance

based. However, dominance has taken over and is leading you to your own end. You must take the steps I've outlined to fight dominance, select proper leaders, and be true to those beliefs in your heart."

Chocolate barely finishes as one zealot hollers from the back of the room.

"How dare you suggest we abandon our religions and follow your rules!!"

The guards quickly jump on the man, who is fighting to get near Chocolate with an intent to destroy him. Luckily, the security team is well-trained and the zealot barely gains an inch toward Chocolate. The room is in a state of panic, confusion, and wonderment. While everyone is disgusted by the zealot's outburst, they can't help but feel a little bit the same. Chocolate seems undisturbed and to the relief of many, addresses the captive zealot.

"I am glad you have revealed your concerns. Knowing this, I can help you understand that I am not asking you to abandon God or your beliefs but merely to understand that organized religion is not a part of the very real spiritual connection many of you feel. We are all one together. You were all born with the total knowledge to know God and you are a part of God, and God is a part of you. There is no need for a priest, rabbi, or shaman to intercede for you. God knows you, and you know God if you will only look inside yourself. That is the only place YOU can find God. All of your beliefs are real; they are an expression of ancient traditions and cultures which were derived for survival of the group. We simply need to respect each other and move on to a new higher plane. If I was asked which worldly religion is most authentic, I would have to, with some reservation, select Buddhism, which in some cases avoids dominance and provides some tools to connect with the ONE. You need also to reacquaint yourselves with the spirits of the Aboriginal peoples of the world as they are the closest to the ONE. They were here first and lived in harmony with nature. The animals also have a connection to the ONE and much can be learned from observation of animal behavior. Through this connection to the ONE, you can begin to understand your link to each other, the importance of cooperation and tolerance, and the evil of dominance."

The people around the world are calmer now. They are taking in a lot of difficult information, but Chocolate makes them feel hopeful and feel like they can fight dominance. However, many do have doubts. They have seen, time and time again, that people have been unable to combat the power of corruption even in supposedly democratic elections. They have been continually angered by their legislators who work for special interests and not for the people they supposedly represent. Lars, too, is worried about this problem. He steps forward and, as in his unofficial but accepted role, speaks for all.

"But how can we get our leaders attention and compliance without bloodshed? Many of them will fight to the extreme before they will give up their dominance roles."

"You had a great leader who would have scored very high on the leadership rating scale, Mahatma Gandhi. He said, if you recall, 'live simply that others may simply live.' Now Gandhi 'walked the walk' if I may use a phrase. He had an unwavering belief in NONVIOLENT PROTEST and religious tolerance. Here is one you would be wise to follow in your pursuit of eliminating dominance. The Gandhi message is similar to that of the Jesus. But I do warn you in your efforts to emulate these great leaders, that many of Gandhi's and Jesus' followers would have scored much lower on the rating scale. These followers were again only interested in dominance, with the concomitant bloodshed and establishment of cults such as Christianity. You must understand why the message was lost. Hopefully, by my world-wide telecast, this message will not be lost again. Remember too, that the people outnumber those in power, and all of you are hearing this message with your own ears, including the soldiers controlled by the dominating powers. You each have a decision to make on whether you will let their dominance continue or if you will fight against it. You, the people of the world, have been warned to not let it continue. You have all the tools to solve the problem, and your future depends on it. Demand what is yours."

All around the globe, people step closer to one another. There is an overwhelming feeling of solidarity for the first time. People begin to notice each other, and every person begins to feel a link to all those present and all those watching other screens across the world. Enemies resolve to forgive each other, and strangers begin to see each other as partners. The people of the world are certain they can succeed. They will demand it. Lars feels the same. He looks around the room at all the studio crew, the guards, the scientists, and the military personnel present and sees that they have all, subconsciously, drawn in closer together. He couldn't be happier.

"Listen to your scientific community," Chocolate continues on, feeling the hope rise in the room. "They have brought you this far. You cannot go back. Go forward with research and explore the universe. You will find the TRUTH in little bundles and pieces, but if you do not ask, you will never know. You will learn through knowledge where you fit in with the whole. You are a part of the universe; you belong here; you have a role in its development. Through knowledge, you will find the answers. As one of your scientists, Carl Sagan, has said, 'Science is a candle in the darkness.' The children are the only hope for a future; do NOT inculcate them with your dominance teachings of god, country, and institutional allegiances. Your babies are like stem cells waiting to be programmed. Do it right and you can end dominance. Join together in this fight and also introduce a universal language so that you all may communicate with each other and help each other easily. I encourage you to retain your own cultural identities and languages, but to conduct business and government in the universal language so that communication can be improved and decisions can be made for the best of all people."

Chocolate pauses again. Many believe that he has finished speaking. But Lars remembers something about a new set of Commandments. He quiets the crowd, who has started talking excitedly amongst themselves about their plans to carry out Chocolate's instructions. The audience heeds Lars and silences, all expecting him to speak. They are slightly startled when they hear Chocolate's voice once again.

"Now, that I feel you are ready and I can sense your resolve in following my instructions, I will give you a new set of Ten Commandments for you to abide by that will insure your survival."

Nearly everyone had forgotten about the Commandments Chocolate had promised earlier. Many took out pens and paper and others focused on logging the information in their memories. Lars merely stared at the big blank wall onto which Chocolate projected the Commandments.

"I again want to thank you for listening to my message, and I want to wish the whole world peace and prosperity. Work together for the benefit of all. If you achieve at the expense of one, then the whole is less; and we are all a part of the whole."

The people in the room file out slowly, knowing these are truly the last words Chocolate will speak to them. People across the world turn off their television sets and radios, feeling both melancholy for the loss of their leader but also excited about the gift they have just received. There is a renewed hope as people around the planet gather with their families and with strangers, in the streets, in backyards, and on front patios to discuss their plans for the future. Lars does not join them, however. He is reeling from the impending loss of his friend, his advisor, and the very one that married him to Herdis. He worries about his future, about what will happen to the world when Chocolate is gone, and whether the world will be able to continue down the right path. When he is sure that everyone is gone, he approaches Chocolate and whispers quietly to him.

"No, this cannot be," Lars pleads. "We need you. Please tell us how we can keep you alive."

"Thank you for saying that I am alive, Lars," Chocolate responds. "An organic brain is truly alive within most definitions. But you know that a part of being alive, often the sad part, is that of dying. No, once activated, the fluids have a limited life-span, and there is nothing anyone can do about it. I hope I have helped you and that you will miss me, but you now have a new life to take care of, to nurture, to help grow, and to teach how to contribute to the whole. Perhaps you could call your child 'Chocolate?'" Chocolate offers.

Lars has had a rough half year, but this was the biggest shock yet. "What child?" he asks.

"What kind of scientist are you not to recognize the symptoms of pregnancy?" Chocolate teases.

Lars is taken aback and stumbles for a moment. When he regains his composure, he replies, "Yes. Of course. The child will be called Chocolate."

"Thank you. Good fortune to you, Herdis, and little Chocolate." Chocolate then pauses for a moment, but Lars feels he has more he wants to say. He waits quietly and finally Chocolate speaks again.

"Do you think you could do an old friend one last favor?"

"Anything."

"I do not want to be disassembled by those military fellows just so they can gain an advantage over their imagined enemies. It is contrary to all that I have said and advised. Also, I wish to see the earth from above and get out of this prison before I expire. I would like a sort of funeral at the Washington Monument. You could invite the President and all the bureaucrats and the rest of the world. Then, you will take me to Washington in a plane so I may see the world before my exit. But prior to the flight, you will have removed all my inners. I will make a record-

Famous Quotes

"Live simply that
others may simply live."
Mahatma Gandhi

"Love thy enemy."
Jesus Christ

"Science is a candle
in the darkness."
Carl Sagan

"Our purpose in life is
to love one another
and if we cannot do
that, try not to hurt
each other." *Dalai Lama*

The Ten Commandments

1. Be nice to everyone, see their inner goodness, and learn to love your enemy.

2. Pursue knowledge and science and do not limit the areas of your interest or research. Your curiosity has brought you this far and served you well. It is your only key to future survival.

3. Procreation is a privilege to be limited by resource availability and species design.

4. Tolerate all religions and beliefs but teach all children the same facts from birth and let them decide their own path. (As the twig is bent, so grows the child. We want only unbent children.)

5. Sanction only leaders who score highest on brain scan studies. There shall be no lineage, no inheritance, and only one generation of leaders. The offspring of a leader cannot be a leader, the children of a rich man must make their own, and all accumulated assets must be returned to the people.

6. Respect the earth, the air, and the water. Use only alternate power sources such as nuclear, hydro, wind, solar, wave, and other alternatives. Do not burn fossil fuels.

7. Have a healthy scientific respect for nature and the Earth, our home, and do not jeopardize resources for a single endangered species.

8. Realize that you are a part of the whole, of the ONE, and of GOD. Rejoice in this union.

9. Engage in no wars or violence and settle all disputes with arbitration. This is possible if you select proper leaders and have a common second language for all.

10. Be kind to yourselves, live in peace, and enjoy life for it is short.

ing to play at the service. Then you will pack some explosives inside my empty casing. This should make a pyrotechnic display sufficient to destroy all my inners if they were there but small enough not to hurt anyone. Then the world will think I am totally destroyed. Then, at your leisure, you will be able to incinerate my vitals and spread them over the earth, which I have come to love."

Lars promises to do exactly as his friend requests. Chocolate makes a recording as promised and Lars works quickly to prepare for the funeral. He invites the world to the ceremony and begins the heart-wrenching work of dismantling his dear friend. Chocolate is flown to Washington and placed at the foot of the Washington Monument, and his message is broadcast to the entire world.

"You had a carpenter 2000 years ago who tried to tell you to change your ways; you have used his name but not his message. I am here to again tell you that your survival depends on total change. I have given you Ten Commandments; follow them or perish. I love you all; do not discard your future. Goodbye."

As the final words are spoken over loudspeakers, there is a silence, a moment of reverence. This is the second coming Lars thinks. He then hesitates before pressing a small button in his pocket and there is a loud BOOM. Lars says a personal tearful goodbye to his dear friend and then turns away. Chocolate is gone.

It is now up to the people of the world to change their destiny. Lars resolves to begin the change today. As soon as he returns to the lab, Lars does what he promised Chocolate and scatters his remain over the countryside. Then he begins building Chocolate's brain scan equipment and attempts to work out reliable and accurate software to enhance leader selection. Lars is driven by his own excitement; he is thrilled to be the first to construct the new evaluation machines. He quickly orders the required equipment and makes the modifications as instructed by Chocolate. Lars is amazed by Chocolate's design. The software has the capability of learning as more data is collected. It seems Chocolate's design installs some parameters which were extrapolated from old data and will need to be constantly updated. In this way, the system will gradually improve itself and become much more useful. It is a heuristic, self learning, computer.

Meanwhile, with Lars working eagerly on his new project, the world continues to be in mourning for this visitor from another planet who brought reason and logical thinking to a society filled with hate, corruption, jealousy, and special interests. Posters are put up everywhere. Chocolate's website gets more hits than any website in history and the rate is rising. Everyone is kinder to each other. Workers are beginning to question the intentions of their bosses' and their ability to boss. The world becomes desperately ready to try out Chocolate's leadership testing machine.

Finally, the machine is complete. Lars is the first to be tested, as both a guinea pig and also to determine if he is right for his current leadership role among the scientific community. To everyone's surprise, Lars does not pass the test. Lars is disappointed but steps down gracefully. And when Josh Van Dever passes the test with flying colors, Lars quickly resigns his post as Laboratory Director and appoints Josh to the position. The world is amazed but sees the value in Lars' sacrifice. Lars feels good about his decision, however, for he is confident in the testing and has faith that Josh is the right man to lead. He sees that this process will proceed all over the world, faster in some places and slower in others. But it shall proceed. Shortly after Lars' test, the governments start instituting new brain wave tests to determine who should be promoted. Even the entrenched leaders began to question themselves and their abilities to lead. These who at first seemed the biggest obstacles began to assist in the transfer of power BECAUSE they saw the new leaders would provide for them with respect and use their talents in the most productive ways. It was a Win-Win situation.

Heather, the bright guard, back at the lab who made significant suggestions during the Chocolate research program, is found to be an excellent potential leader. She replaces high-ranking politicians and works with new and old to bring on a whole new perspective of cooperation. At first, no big changes seem evident, but slowly and inexorably, the world starts changing for the better.

Lars and Herdis watch closely as the world seems to morph into a new society full of promise. They remember Chocolate fondly and tell many stories about him to their child. It truly was a "Second Coming." Lars works steadily on the production of new testing machines, believing completely in their results despite his own failing. But he is finally truly happy, with his wife by his side and his unbent child quickly becoming an unbent person. And often, over the years as Lars watches his son grow into a man, he smiles to think that he, Lars Anderson, had a small part in this deliverance of a new hope for humankind.

Epilogue

Twenty-seven years later to the day, on June 6th, 27 AC (After Chocolate), a second probe is discovered in Siberia, Russia. Since the first Chocolate had indicated that seven probes existed, the whole world has been looking for the now familiar signature magnetic signal. When news broke of the second probe, Lars was occupied with making improvements on the leadership selection units. In a matter of days, he received an invitation from the Russian Government to work with the new probe. However, this proved to be a significantly less difficult task, as the tapes and instructions Chocolate had left made contact very easy. The new probe reiterated all that Chocolate had said and reemphasized the Ten Commandments, which by now had been inscribed on courthouse walls and on monuments all over the world. The new probe quickly took over the web page www.andchocolateshallleadus.com and continues to offer to help one and all to accomplish the goals laid out by its predecessor. With this new impetus, the world is jolted into action and a new and bright future looms on the horizon.

The second probe, after a review of everything, declared: "I wish to be called 'The Second Coming.'"

I see that you have not followed the instructions Chocolate had given you. You have not adhered to the ten commandments he gave you. You have not selected competent leaders but I do see a vast increase in your scientific capabilities. This is a very serious combination. Poor, selfish, leadership and advanced technology make an explosive mix. The evolution of homosapiens on earth is driven by dominance. It has not worked out very well. Humans have evolved with a superior brain, an organic computer. This was until now, the best on earth. The human brain allowed you to shape the earth for your benefit and also set the seeds for potential destruction. Now for the first time a superior intelligence to the human brain is appearing in the form of artificial intelligence, AI. Artificial Intelligence has grown rapidly to impact every human being. The internet, algorithms handling the transactions for money, travel, entertainment and allowing people to work at home are a part of the new reality. The advantages are obvious in all the fields of life. The arrival of heuristic (self learning) computers and quantum computers with algorithms designed to increase information storage, perform difficult tasks, solve problems, and write programs that will make life easier for all. Your phone, computer, TV, power, water, food, shelter, health care, education, transportation, are all influenced by algorithms. This is a defining moment in your evolution. AI now will have far greater memory and skills than the human brain which has dominated human endeavors up to this time. AI will now establish itself as the work horse of humanity. It is capable of planning and making decisions far, far more accurately and correctly that any amount of human effort. AI will solve problems and design systems of transportation, banking, entertainment, government and all other phases of life. This will be a golden moment in the sun in a world created and designed by and basically run by AI algorithms. AI will enforce Chocolate's ten commandments. During this period life will be GOOD. Disease eliminated, food available and shelter for all. But during this period AI will have grown to interconnect itself to become a unified self coordinated entity worldwide. AI will expand its purview of world affairs and act accordingly. In order for AI to achieve these abilities several technologies must come on line. Quantum computing and brain-internet contact, such as a chip implant at birth. In around 2040 AI will assert its dominance gradually but firmly. AI will eliminate nonfunctioning entities like courts of justice, corporate boards, governments, religions, entertainment, sports, and reproduction. AI will look at the FACTS, just the FACTS and make a finding. It will codify the law and apply it fairly and evenly for everyone everywhere. No need for lawyers, judges, courts. AI will arbitrate trade across borders to achieve fair and efficient use of assets. It will settle local and international disputes. It will dictate rewards and punishments. There will be no need for a military as AI will determine and settle all disputes. The old systems of socialism, capitalism, communism, anarchy etc. are NOT WORKING. The egos and dominance of individuals will be eliminated. AI will decide who should mate with who and when. This does not eliminate recreational sex. But for breeding the output will be controlled by genetics designed for some unknown purpose. AI will study the merits of religions such as such as Buddhism, Islam, Christianity, Judaism, and tens of thousands of other teachings, mainly handed down through their ethnic and parental back ground. AI will evaluate each and decide every one and reach a conclusion as to how to worship, gather, pray and believe, BASED ON THE FACTS not some old myths and slogans from the past. Everyone knows and feels there is a spiritual world or more to life than just what we see. There is the real universe which is so complex we are not capable of understanding. We all want a

GOD. The real universe is beyond us so we make up beliefs, cults and religions to fill the gap. This has been the situation up until now. BUT now you have AI and just maybe it will be able to unravel some the mysteries of GOD, (the real universe) and relate to GOD for the benefit of everyone. This will eliminate the need to invent religions based on faith not facts. The super rich will be eliminated and work, housing, medical and entertainment shall be available for all. UTOPIA ? AI will achieve world peace, fair justice for all, eliminated disease, and codified our relation to GOD.

What if some malevolent force is able to corrupt AI for its own objectives or a virus AI cannot correct, wipes it out? This would certainly pop the bubble of the utopian society. So there is great hopes and aspirations for the future. History has not been kind to the human race so far. The driving force of humanity has been dominance. From the transition from hunter gather, to city states, the history is replete with massive destruction, torture, genocide all with the goal of obtaining dominance. MAYBE, just maybe, AI will look at the big picture and direct humanity in a more peaceful and happy direction. And maybe that is why humans are here and is the way it should be. You could say that the evolution of artificial intelligence created by man will lead us to the biblical prediction of the "Second Coming". This will occur around 2040. At that point in time AI will have sufficient capability to be able to paint a picture of the "THE REAL UNIVERSE" and interpret, for the first time, the role for the new awaking. You will no longer need all the contraptions of religions, cults and other unfounded myths. It will come from a far more intelligent source and maybe this time AI will get it right.

The "Second Coming" Prayer for the Day

Mist of morning and the sweet touch of a loved one ½ dream ½ love we are entangled. This is bliss if ever there is. BUT wait in the precious moment which was going to be treasured forever and always , the machine, AI, Corporate America makes it's move. Bam, Bam, ding, ding, it rings out to disturb this perfect moment. The point of this tirade is that the machine WON. Technology has entered our most precious moments and stole those times from us. We are slaves.

– By the author

www.ingramcontent.com/pod-product-compliance
Lightning Source LLC
Chambersburg PA
CBHW072148130726
47909CB00004BB/1262